THE MUMMY CASE

////

J.R. RAIN

JIM KNIGHTHORSE SERIES

Published by
Crop Circle Books
212 Third Crater, Moon

Printed in the United States of America.

ISBN: 9781723971297

1.

I was doing decline push ups when my office door opened. Decline push ups cause a lot of blood to rush to your head and a fabulous burn across the upper pectorals. They also looked pretty damn silly in a professional environment. Luckily, this wasn't a professional environment.

Somebody was quietly watching me, probably admiring my near-perfect form or the way my tee shirt rippled across my broad shoulders. Either way, I rattled off twenty more, completing my set of a hundred.

In a distinctive country twang, a man's voice said, "I could come back."

"And miss my near-perfect form?"

I eased my running shoes off the desk and immediately felt a wave of light-headedness. Granted, I didn't entirely mind the light-headedness. I am, after all, a sucker for a good buzz.

The man who came swimmingly into view was wearing a cowboy hat and leaning against my door frame, a bemused expression on his weathered face. He was about twenty years my senior.

"Howdy partner," I said.

He tipped his Stetson. "So what are those push ups supposed to do, other than cause a lot of blood rush to your head?"

"That's enough for me," I said happily. "Oh, and they happen to be a hell of a chest work-out."

"Seems like a lot of trouble," he said.

"It's not easy being beautiful."

"Ah," he said. "You must be Jim Knight-horse. I heard about you."

"Lucky you."

As he spoke, his Adam's apple bobbed up and down like a buoy in a storm. His white hat sported an excessively rolled brim—completely useless now against the sun or rain. Maybe he was a country music star.

"I was told you could be a cocky son of a bitch."

"You would be, too," I said. "If you were me."

He looked at me and shrugged. "Well, maybe. You're certainly a big son of a bitch."

I said nothing. My size spoke for itself. He looked around my small office, perhaps noting the many pictures and trophies that cluttered the walls and bookcases, all in recognition of my considerable prowess on the football field. Actually, all but one. There was a second place spelling bee trophy in there somewhere. Lost it on *zumbooruk*, a camel-mounted canon used in the Middle East. Hell of a shitty word to lose it on.

"I heard you could help me," he said finally, almost pitifully.

"Ah," I said. "Have a seat."

He did, moseying on into my small office. As he sat, I almost expected him to flip the client chair around and straddle it backward, cowboy-like. Instead, he used the chair as it was originally designed, although it was clearly not designed for someone as tall as he. His bony knees reached up to his ears and looked sharp enough to cut through his denim jeans. I sat behind the desk in a leather brass-studded chair that was entirely too ornate for its surroundings.

The leather made rude noises.

Ever the professional detective, I kept a straight face and asked for his name.

"Jones," he answered. "*Jones T. Jones*, to be exact."

"That's a lot of Joneses."

"Well, yes," he said, blushing slightly. "It's not really my name, you see. It's sort of like a stage name. You know, a gimmick."

"So you're an actor?"

"No, I own a souvenir shop in Huntington Beach. But I've acted as the spokesperson in my own commercials." Ah. It came to me then. I'd seen Jones before, late at night on the local cable circuit. Usually right before I passed out in a drunken stupor. Damn cheesy commercials, too, many involving what appeared to be a rabid monkey. Sometimes Jones and the monkey danced. I was embarrassed for Jones. "Maybe you've heard of it," he continued. "Ye Olde Curiosity Shoppe."

"Heard of it?" I said. "Hell, I spelled *old* and *shop* with extra *e's* and *p's* up until the fifth grade. My teacher, Mrs. Franks, thought I was Chaucer reborn."

He laughed. "I wanted to change the name when I bought the store a number of years ago, but there was a big public uproar." He cracked a smile, and I realized that he *enjoyed* the big public uproar. "So I gave in to pressure and kept the damn name. I regret it to this day."

"Why?"

"No one can find us in the phone book...or even on the internet. They call us and ask: Are we under *Y* or *O*? Is it *Ye* or *The*?" He sighed and caught his breath, having worked himself up. "I mean, what were the original owners thinking?"

"Maybe they were English."

He shrugged. We were silent. Outside, in the nearby alley, a delivery truck was backing up, beeping away. I was one of the few people who appreciated the warning beeps.

"So what can I do for you, Mr. Jones?" I asked.

"I'd like to hire you."

"*Zumbooruk!*" I said.

"Excuse me?"

"Exactly."

J.R. RAIN

2.

"You know about Sylvester the Mummy, then?" asked Jones.

"Still dead?" I asked.

"As a doornail."

Sylvester the Mummy was one of Huntington Beach's main attractions—ranking a distant third behind *waves* and *babes*—and currently resided at the back of the Ye Olde Curiosity Gift Shoppe in a cozy polyurethane case for all the world to see. Sylvester had been found in the California deserts over a hundred years ago near a ghost town called Rawhide. Since then, he'd been passed from museum to museum, exhibit to exhibit, until finally coming to rest at Ye Olde Gift Shoppe in Huntington Beach. Wouldn't his mother be proud? Although his identity is unknown, most historians figure Sylvester had once been a cowboy. Which, I figure, means he probably once owned a horse and a six shooter, ate beans from the can over an open campfire and sang lonesome songs about loose women. That is, of course, until someone put a bullet in his gut and left him for dead in the middle of the Mojave Desert. Experts figured the old boy had mummified within 24 hours due to a rare combination of extreme desert heat and chemicals in the sand. A true John Doe, he had been named after the very miner who discovered him, which I always found a little creepy.

"What about him?" I asked.

"Two months ago, as a publicity stunt, I hired a young historian fresh out of college to look into Sylvester's background. You know, generate some interest in my little store. Of course, I didn't really think the historian would find anything on Sylvester. But that wasn't the point."

"The point being to generate interest in your little store."

"Yes, exactly."

Ah, exploiting the dead.

"Go on," I said.

Jones shifted, suddenly looking uncomfortable, as if his tight jeans were giving him one hell of a wedgie. "The historian—a kid really—provided me regular reports. He did original research, digging through old records, even traveling out to Rawhide once or twice to interview the town historian."

He stopped talking. I waited. I sensed something ominous. I call this my sixth sense. Catchy, huh?

Jones' expression turned pained. The mother of all wedgies? "Then the reports stopped, and I didn't hear from him for a while. Shortly thereafter, his mother reported him missing. Soon after that, the sheriff's department found him dead."

"Found him where?"

"In the desert. Near Rawhide." He took a deep breath. "And just this morning I received word from the San Bernardino Sheriff's Department that his death was being officially ruled an accident. They figure he got lost in the desert, ran out of gas and died of thirst."

I sat back in my chair and rested my chin on my fingertips. Sweat had appeared on Jones's forehead. His flashy showmanship was out the window.

"I assume you disagree with their findings," I said.

He thought about it.

"I suppose so, yes."

"Why?"

He reached up and unconsciously rolled the brim of his Stetson, a nervous habit, which now explained why the thing looked like a Del Taco Macho Burrito.

My stomach growled. Lord help me.

"It's hard to say, Knighthorse. It's just a gut feeling I have. The kid...the kid was smart, you know. A recent college graduate. I was impressed by him, and not just by his book smarts. He seemed to have a sensible head on his shoulder; street smarts, too."

"Too sensible to get lost in the desert."

"Yes. Precisely. That's exactly why I'm here."

"That," I said, "and you feel guilty as hell for sending a kid out to his death."

He looked away, inhaled deeply. "Jesus, Knighthorse. Put it that way, and you make it seem like *I* killed him."

"So what do you want me to do?"

"I want you to look into his death. Make sure it was an accident."

"And if it wasn't an accident?"

"I want you to find the killer."

"Finding the killer is extra."

"Price is no object."

"Zumbooruk!"

"Why do you keep saying that? What does it mean?"

"It's a camel-mounted canon used in the Middle East."

"I don't get it."

"Neither do I."

J.R. RAIN

3.

I met Detective Sherbet at a sandwich shop on Amerige St. in downtown Fullerton. Sherbet was a big man with a big cop mustache. He wore an old blue suit and a bright yellow tie. He ordered coffee and a donut. I ordered a Diet Pepsi, but thought the donut idea was a pretty good one. So I had the waitress bring me three of whatever she had left, because when it comes to donuts, any flavor will do.

"What if she brings you a pink donut?" asked Detective Sherbet.

"Pink is good," I said.

"I hate pink."

"In general?"

He thought about that, then nodded. "Yeah." He paused, looked away. "My boy likes pink."

"I'm sorry," I said.

"Me, too."

"How old is your boy?"

"Eight."

"Maybe he will grow out of it."

"Let's hope."

The waitress brought me three cake donuts. Chocolate, glazed, and pink.

Uh oh.

"Are you okay with me eating this?" I asked, pointing to Sherbet's arch-nemesis, the pink-frosted donut.

He nodded, shrugging. The man had serious issues. I ate the pink donut quickly, nonetheless. As I did, Sherbet watched me curiously, as if I was a monkey in a zoo exhibiting strange behavior. Funny, when I was done, I didn't feel gay.

"Any good?" he asked.

"Quite," I said. "And no gay side effects. At least not yet."

"Maybe I'll have one."

And he did. One pink donut. After the waitress set it before him, he picked it up warily with his thumb and forefinger, careful of the pink frosting. He studied it from a few angles, and then bit into it.

"Your son would be proud," I said.

"I love the kid."

"But you think he might be gay."

"Let's change the subject," he said.

"Thankfully," I said. Actually, Detective Sherbet wasn't so much homophobic as *homoterrified*, as in terrified his kid might grow up to be gay. Someone needed some counseling here, and it wasn't the kid.

"So that crackpot hired you," said Sherbet. There was pink frosting in the corner of his mouth. Lord, he looked gay.

"Crackpot being Jones T. Jones."

"A shyster if I've ever met one. Anything to make a buck. Hell, I even had my suspicions that he offed the historian just to generate more press for that damn store of his. Have you been there?"

I nodded.

He said, "Place gives me the fucking creeps."

"So he's clean?"

"Sure he's clean. Everyone's clean. Kid ran out of gas, wandered around the desert until he died of heat and thirst."

"Hell of a way to go."

Sherbet shrugged, and as he did so his mustache twitched simultaneously. Perhaps the motor neurons in his shoulders were connected to his upper lip.

"I hear Willie was a smart kid," I said.

Sherbet nodded. "Smart enough to get a Masters in history from UCI."

"Probably smart enough to call for help on his cell phone."

"Sure," said Sherbet, "except he didn't have one on him."

"Who found his body?"

"San Bernardino Sheriff. They found the body and called me out, as I was working the original missing person case. We compared notes, asked around, decided this thing was nothing but an accident. We both closed our cases."

"Have you talked to anyone at Rawhide?" I asked.

"Sure, went out there with the San Bernardino Sheriff. We asked around, talked to the museum curator and his assistant, the last two to see Willie alive."

"What did they say?"

Sherbet shrugged again. His shoulders were probably hairy. Sherbet was a very manly man, which was probably why he couldn't comprehend his kid turning out gay.

"Like I said, they were the last two to see

Willie alive, at least that we know of. The museum curator and his assistant—forget their names now—showed him the site where that fucking mummy was originally found. Afterward, when everyone left the site, Willie was in his own truck right behind the curator and assistant. They look again, and Willie's gone. They assumed he headed home in a different direction. Both their stories corroborate. Granted, this is an oddball way for a bright kid to die, but unless something rears its ugly head here, we have no reason to suspect any funny business."

I drank some Diet Pepsi. I'm not even really convinced that I like Diet Pepsi. I took another sip; nope, still not convinced.

"Jones seems to think there was foul play," I said. "And gave me a hefty retainer fee to prove it."

"Jones wants business. Twenty bucks says he turns this thing into an even bigger circus. He's the ring leader, and you're the...." He paused, thinking.

"World's Strongest Man?" I offered.

"Sure, whatever. Look, I think he's using you, Knighthorse. Especially you, since you have some name recognition."

"Did you want my autograph for your kid?" I asked.

"You kidding? Kid doesn't know a fullback

from a backpack." Sherbet shook his head some more, sipped his coffee. "All this over a fucking mummy."

"Hard to believe."

4.

It was a warm Saturday afternoon and Cindy and I were jogging along the beach with, perhaps, two billion other people. We used the bike path that ran parallel to the ocean, expertly dodging dog walkers, roller bladers, baby strollers, various shapes and sizes of humans and, of course, bikes.

Cindy was dressed in black Spandex running pants and a long-sleeved shirt that said O'Neil on the back in blue script. She was the only human being within five square miles wearing a long-sleeved shirt. She had also smeared blue gunk over the bridge of her nose and along her cheekbones, which made her look like a wide receiver, minus the helmet and cup. I was dressed only in knee length shorts and running shoes. No shirt, no sunscreen, no blue gunk. No problem.

"That blue gunk is scaring the kids," I said.

"That blue gunk, as you call it, is sunscreen, and it helps to keep me looking young."

"You're thirty-one. That's young enough."

"But I want to look twenty-one."

As we jogged, we spoke easily, casually. Cindy huffed or puffed once or twice. I don't huff or puff, although I was very conscious of a dull ache in my right leg, a leg held together by stainless steel pins and will power. Superman has his kryptonite; I have my stainless steel pins.

"So if you can stay ten years ahead of the aging curve you would be happy?" I said.

"Ecstatic."

"There are women who would kill to look thirty-one."

"You think I look thirty-one?"

Oops. So what was the old formula? Add two inches, subtract four years? "You easily look twenty-seven."

"Twenty-seven? How the hell did you come

up with that number?"

"It's a formula."

"Formula?"

"Never mind."

"So how old do I really look to you?" she asked.

"Definitely not thirty-one," I said. "How about early twenties?"

"Then why did you say twenty-seven?"

"Twenty-seven on a bad day."

"I have bad days?"

"Not as bad as I'm having."

She looked at me, and I think she was smiling somewhere under the blue gunk. She patted my backside. "Sorry I'm being hard on you. I'm just finding aging and wrinkles hard to deal with."

We passed a row of sunbathers who had ventured maybe five feet from the bike path out onto the sand. They were still a good fifty yards from the water. Maybe they were afraid of sharks.

"I say wear your age like a badge of honor," I said.

"I would prefer not to wear a badge of wrinkles, thank you very much. Look at all these women, Jim. They're all so young, and beautiful and smooth-skinned. And most of them are looking at you. Could you please put your shirt back on."

"I'm working on my tan."

"Work on it somewhere else. Besides, you're burning."

"Part of the process. I happen to be Caucasian."

"Women are ogling you."

"Ogling is bad?"

"Only when I'm feeling old."

I slipped my tank top back on, which had been tucked in the waistband of my shorts. Cindy looked me over, shook her head. "Somehow you look even better."

"Maybe I should quit lifting weights."

"Would you do that for me?"

"Don't push it."

We stopped at Balboa Pier. I bought two bottles of water from a street vendor and briefly eyeballed a dehydrated hot dog until Cindy pulled me away. We found an empty bench and seized it. Our knees touched, which sent a thrill of pleasure coursing through me, all over again.

"You thrill me," I said.

She looked at me from over her water bottle. "Even after eight years?"

"I've spent eight years being fascinated. Not too many people can say that."

She smiled and took hold of my sweaty hand. My sweat never bothered her, the surest sign of true love. Cindy's nails were painted red. I love red nails, and she knew it. The brighter the better, since I'm certifiably color blind.

"Explain to me again why you agreed to look into the historian's death."

I found her blue nose heavily distracting. I wanted to taste it.

"Because it's what I do," I said. "Sometimes I go days without work; hell, and sometimes even weeks. So when someone walks in through my door and hands me a check to investigate something, I would be foolish not to."

"Even if this someone is using you for his own self-promotion?"

I shook my head. "Jones and I have an agreement: no self-promotion while I'm on the case. Besides, if I were to disapprove of the motives of every client prior to taking a case, I would be homeless and hungry."

"But the police have ruled the historian's death an accident."

"The police are often overworked."

"And you are not?"

"Not often enough," I said. "A private investigator can spend more time on a case, work it more thoroughly, perhaps bend a few laws here and there to find answers in places the police are not willing or able to look. Not a bad way to go if you are unsatisfied with the answers you are given."

"And Jones is unsatisfied."

"Yes."

"I think he's feeling guilty," she said.

"I agree."

"But you don't care about his motives."

"Not enough to turn down honest work."

"Honest?"

"Honest enough."

"You think there might be something to this case?" she asked.

"Jones seems to think so, and that's enough for me."

"You'll take the money and job, of course, because that's what you do," she said, looking at me. "But on another level you can't wait to dig into this case, see what you turn up."

"One never knows."

"So what's your first step?"

"Cash Jones's check and pay my rent."

"And then what?"

"Buy some food, maybe even a foot massager for you. Wink, wink."

She slapped my hand. "Focus."

"I'll probably give the mummy a visit. You know, immerse myself in the case and all that. Want to come?"

She shuddered. "I've always hated that thing."

"That 'thing' is a murdered man," I said.

She suddenly turned to me.

"I knew it!" she said excitedly.

"Knew what?"

"This isn't just about the historian."

I crossed my arms and grinned. "It's not?"

"No."

"So tell me what it's about."

She was facing me, excited. "You're going to figure out who this mummy was."

"Go on."

"Even more, you're going to find his killer, or die trying, because that's the way you are. You help those in need, even if they're hundred-year-old mummies."

"Mummies need justice too," I said.

She looked at me for perhaps twenty seconds, and, although I could have been wrong, there seemed to be real love in her eyes. Who could blame her.

"Yes," she said finally, laying her head on my shoulder. "They certainly do."

We sat like that for ten minutes, enjoying each other's silence, enjoying the parade of humanity, enjoying the sights and sounds and smells of the ocean. I noticed men looking at Cindy's pretty face, somehow seeing beyond the blue gunk to the real beauty beneath. But then they got a look at me and moved on.

***

We were walking back to my place along the boardwalk, hand-in-hand. The sun was hot on my neck and a nearby seagull, balancing precariously on a low brick wall, was working on a tightly crumpled Subway wrapper. Maybe it was on the Jared diet.

"Someone vandalized my office," Cindy suddenly said.

The words had the same effect as a punch to the solar plexus. I stopped walking and faced her.

"Vandalized how?"

"Trashed my lecture hall. Turned over anything they could get their hands on. Graffitied everything."

"Are the campus police on it?"

"Yeah."

"Any leads?"

"Creationists."

"Creationists?"

"Or anti-Darwinists," she said. To her students, Cindy was known as Professor Darwin. And, yes, she was the great great granddaughter of the infamous Charles, his bloodline living to this day, which says a little something about surviving and fitness and all that. She continued, "They spray-painted crosses and fishes on the walls and chalk boards. Even left me a message on my computer screen."

"What Would Jesus Do?"

"No," she said. "'Darwin is burning in hell, and so will you.'"

"Not if he has his great great granddaughter's penchant for sunscreen."

"Not funny. I'm scared. This wasn't your typical prank. I've dealt with those my entire life." She took in some air, looked down at her half-filled water bottle. "There was a lot of anger involved in this attack. A lot. You could see it, feel it."

"You want me to look into it?"

We started walking again. She slipped her hands around my right bicep, her fingertips not quite able to touch. She was beautiful and petite and I wanted to hug her but I was afraid of getting blue stuff on my white tank top.

"Yeah," she said. "They scared me."

They scared her. I involuntarily tightened my hand into a fist. My bicep swelled before her thunderstruck eyes. I could feel the hair on my neck standing up. Hackles.

"Yeah," I said, "I'll look into it."

J.R. RAIN

5.

It was late and I was drinking alone on my balcony, feet up on the railing, gazing out across the empty black expanse that was the Pacific Ocean. The night air was cold, laced heavily with salt brine. The moon tonight was hidden behind a heavy layer of stratus clouds. A 12-pack of Bud Light was sitting on the balcony between my feet like an obedient dog.

Good doggy.

It was the first beer I had bought in six months. Hell, the first I had tasted in six months.

And it tasted heavenly.

Too heavenly.

I was in trouble.

Twenty-one years ago my mother had been murdered. As a ten-year-old boy, I had found her dead in her bedroom in a pool of her own blood. Her throat had been slashed and she had been raped. Her murderer was never found. A cold case, if ever there was one.

Six months ago my father handed over a packet of forgotten photographs of my mother, taken on the last day that she was alive on this earth. Other than being of obvious sentimental interest to me, the photos contained the one and only clue to her murder. At least, I hoped.

The clue: a random young man in the background of three of the twenty-four photographs. In the three photographs, he appears to be stalking her—at least that's what my gut tells me. And I've learned to listen to my gut.

I drank some more beer. I prefer bottles, but cans leave less evidence—no bottles caps showing up in seat cushions, for instance—and less evidence is what I preferred, at least for now.

From the glass patio table, I picked up one of the three pictures of the young man in question; the young man who may or may not have been stalking my parents; the young man who may or may not have murdered my mother.

That's a big leap, I thought.

True, but a big leap was all I had.

I angled the picture until it caught some of the ambient light from the street below. There he was, holding a freshly caught sandshark, standing behind my parents, themselves standing on the Huntington Beach pier. His hair was ragged and longish, bleached blond from hours in the sun and salt. He was wearing a red tank top and longish shorts, although not as long as the shorts kids wear today. His right leg was tanned and well muscled, although I could only see a fraction of it. My father obscured the rest of his body. *Thanks, dad. Asshole.* The young man was laughing at the rabbit ears my mother was not-so-secretly giving my father.

I set the picture down again. Inhaled deeply, looked up at the swirling mass of clouds above.

He had taken an interest in my mother, that much was evident. Probably because my mother made him laugh. Probably because she was a striking woman. Perhaps she had fascinated him. Perhaps he had always fantasized about being with an older woman. She was a striking woman. He himself was good-looking and muscular in that surfer sort of way. Whereas I was muscular in that strong-looking way.

The beer I was holding was miraculously empty. Wasn't sure how that happened, barely even remembered drinking it. I opened another.

My mother's case had been thoroughly inv-estigated and was later shelved due to lack of evidence. Hell, lack of *anything*. I remembered the homicide detective. A good man who was deeply troubled by my mother's murder. During his investigation, he had spoken to me often, once or twice even taking me out to get ice cream. I think he knew my father was an ass-hole.

But now I had these....

Pictures. Evidence.

Something.

I finished the beer, placed the empty tin car-cass on the glass table and popped open another one.

I had grown up in a tough part of Inglewood. We had been poor in those days, my father was fresh out the military and not very family-orien-ted, if his nightly liaisons with the neighbor-hood whores were any indication. By the age of ten, I had witnessed a half dozen murders and more robberies than I cared to count. Growing up, I thought bullet-riddled bodies lying on street corners were sights that all school kids saw on their way home from school. Probably not the best neighborhood to raise a kid and my mother knew this. To escape, she took me to the beach any chance she had. She loved Huntington Beach, especially the pier. We would sit for hours overlooking the ocean. Sometimes I would fish, but mostly we ate ice creams and I told her about my day.

The same pier she was at in these pictures. The same pier I could see from my balcony.

Another empty can of beer. How the hell did that happen? I opened another and pondered this mystery.

Later, when the 12-pack was finally gone, I gathered up the empty cans in a trash bag and deposited the whole thing down the trash chute, and unwrapped a candy mint and lay down on my bed. My bladder was full. The ceiling spun. I awoke the next morning with the mint stuck to my forehead. Nice. My bladder was even fuller.

Between my thumb and forefinger, held in a sort of vice-like deathgrip, was the picture of the young man standing behind my mother.

J.R. RAIN

6.

Ye Olde Curiosity Shoppe, with its extra *e's* and *p's,* was located just a half mile from my apartment. I could have walked there, but decided to drive, because nobody walks in Orange County, either.

The building itself was made of cinder block, painted in a red and white checkerboard pattern. White stars were painted within the red squares. It looked like a nightclub or an ice rink.

The time was noon, and the store had just opened. Inside, the curiosity shop was filled with, well, curiosities. Most of it was junk, and most of it was designed to lure away the tourist's buck. I passed rows of shrunken heads, tribal spears, bobble heads and postcards. California license plate key chains with names like Dwayne, LaToya and Javier.

The store itself was smallish, made smaller by the overwhelming amount of junk. Inventory must have been hell. I was the only customer in the store. No surprise there, as it had just opened.

I headed to the rear of the store, side-stepping a curtain of crystal talismans, and there was the old boy. Sealed within a polyurethane case, Sylvester stood guard next to a door marked Employees Only. I wondered if he was on the clock.

I stepped up to the case.

Sylvester was not a handsome man. His skin was blackened and shriveled. His lips had disappeared in the mummification process, and so had most of his eyes. His hair was there, but short and scraggly. You would think, after all these years, someone would have thought to brush it. He was naked, although his genitalia had shriveled and disappeared. My heart went out to him. His hands were crossed under his stomach, the same position he was found in a hundred years ago.

I had aged twenty-five years since the first time I had seen Sylvester; he didn't appear a day older. Mummification has that effect.

According to the legend at the base of the pedestal, Sylvester stood six feet one inches and weighed nearly two hundred pounds. His identity was unknown. His killer unknown. The hole was there, above his right wrist, clear as day. No bullet had been found, as it had exited out his back, shot clean through. A shot that had torn up his insides and caused him to bleed to death in the desert.

The storeroom door opened, startling me slightly. Sylvester ignored the door, and ignored me for the most part. A kid came out, smiled at me, looked casually at the dead man in the case, and then headed toward the cash registers.

"Not very talkative." I nodded toward Sly.

"He's a mummy," said the employee.

"Ah, would explain it."

The kid didn't seem to care much that the man in the case had been murdered.

But I cared. Hell, I was being paid to care. Sort of. And the more I thought of it, the more I cared.

I reread the legend for the dozenth time. Sylvester had been found in the California desert, near Rawhide, now known as the Rawhide Ghost Town. Historians had found no evidence as to who he was or why he was killed. After his discovery, Sylvester had been passed from museum to museum, paraded around until this day. The only justification as to why he was not given a proper burial was that he was a mummy, and therefore of interest to science and history.

Now he was just of interest to Jones's pocketbook.

I stepped up next to the case, my face just inches from Sly's own. I stared at him, soaking in the details of his dried-out face, his half-open eyes, and his shriveled remains of a nose. I stared at him, and we played the blinking game for a half a minute. He won, although he might have flinched.

I put my hand on the case.

Well, buddy, I think you are more than a freak show curiosity. I think you were once a person, a person who died a hell of a shitty death. I care that you suffered so much. I care that you bled to death. I care that you never got that last drink of water you so desperately craved. Of course, you didn't leave me much to go on, but that's never stopped me before. But first I have to look into the death of a young historian, who may or may not have died accidentally. Maybe you know him. I hear he was a good kid. His name is Willie Clarke.

"There's no touching the display," said the voice of the employee behind me. "Now that we serve ice cream here, I'm always cleaning off sticky fingerprints. It's a pain in my ass. I'm sure you understand."

"Of course," I said, and left.

J.R. RAIN

.

7.

The University of Irvine police sub-station was a single story wooden structure located on the outskirts of campus. A female officer in her twenties was working the front desk. She had on a cop uniform from the waist up, and cop shorts from the waist down. Her legs were thick and well muscled. Nothing says sexy like cop shorts.

She asked if I was here to pay a parking ticket. I showed her my P.I. license and told her who I was and what I was doing here. Without looking at the license, she told me to wait. I snapped my wallet shut. Her loss; she missed a hell of a picture. She disappeared through a back door.

I struck a jaunty pose at the counter and waited, ankles crossed, weight on one elbow. Surveyed the room. Wasn't much to survey. Typical campus sub-station was designed mostly to accept payments for parking tickets, which, I think, funded much of UCI's scientific research. Behind the counter were a few empty desks, the occupants probably out giving more parking tickets.

Soon enough I was sitting at a small desk watching a small cop eating a bowl of Oriental noodles. Judging by the way that he recklessly slurped, he seemed irritated that I disturbed his meal. His name was Officer Baker.

"Caught me on a lunch break," he said, wiping his mouth carefully with a folded napkin.

"I hadn't realized."

"Professor Darwin said you might come by, and if you did, to fill you in with what's going on."

"She knows I worry."

"Quite frankly, I'm a little worried, too."

In my lap, I realized I had balled my hands into fists. My knuckles were showing white, crisscrossed with puffy scars from too many fights everywhere. Grade school, high school, college. Just last week. My fists were wide, a hell of a knuckle sandwich.

"Any leads?" I asked.

"None."

"Any other professors targeted?"

He shook his head. "No. Just Professor Darwin."

"Did the surveillance cameras catch anything?"

He briefly eyeballed his noodles. "No."

"Any witnesses?"

"Again, no."

I inhaled, wondering what, if anything, had been done about this.

"How about protection for Professor Darwin?"

"We offered to escort her across campus, but she declined. She said she has pepper spray and wasn't afraid to use it. And that you had taught her self-defense." He was a really small man, made smaller by the fact that he had yet to do anything for Cindy. He sat forward in his desk. "I know you are concerned. But I am personally looking into this. We patrol Professor Darwin's office, her lecture hall, and her car regularly. I assure you, sooner rather than later, we will find this creep."

"You have any objections if I come by a few

nights a week and poke around?"

He looked at me. "You the same Knighthorse who played for UCLA?"

"One and only."

"Then I have no objections," he said.

I left his office. Sometimes it's good to be me.

8.

Cindy and I finished our Saturday morning jog at the beach, ending up at my place. To conserve water, we showered together. Zowie! Cindy scrubbed the blue gunk off her face, and then tried her best to scrub me off her. She succeeded with the former but not the latter. Now we were at the Huntington Beach Brew Pub, surrounded by a lot of beer in huge stainless steel vats. *A lot* of beer.

A waitress came by carrying three sloshing ice-encrusted mugs in one hand by their ice-encrusted handles to a nearby table. I watched her carefully. Or, more accurately, the beer carefully.

"I hope it's okay that we're here," Cindy said.

"I'll be fine."

"But you've been doing so well lately. I hate to tempt you like this."

"Actually, not as well as you think." I looked her in the eye, took a deep breath. "And you probably shouldn't feel very proud."

She was in the act of raising her glass of water to her lips. It stopped about halfway. "You've been drinking again."

"Yes."

"How much?"

"Not as much."

She set the glass back down. Perhaps a little too loudly. Our waitress picked that moment to come by, asked if we were ready to order. I shook my head and said no, keeping my eyes on Cindy.

When the waitress was gone, Cindy said, "Jim, you promised you would quit."

"I quit for nearly three months. A record for me."

"So what happened?"

"Turns out the more I look into my mother's murder, the more I want to drink."

Her mouth was tight. She kept her hands still on the table. She took a deep breath, looked down at her hands. She was thinking, coming to some sort of decision. "And you said you haven't been drinking as much as before."

"That's true."

"At least that's something."

"Yes."

"And you have been able to control the drinking?"

"More so than before."

"Do you need help?"

"Probably."

"But you don't want it."

"Not yet."

The waitress came by again. This time she saw us talking and didn't bother to stop.

"You have a problem," Cindy said.

"I know."

"How long have you been drinking?"

"A few weeks now."

"Thank you for telling me."

I shrugged. "Should have told you sooner."

"But you told me. I know it's not easy. I don't want you to hide it from me."

"It's not something I'm proud of."

"I know. So what are you going to do about it?"

"For now, nothing."

"So you'll keep drinking?"

"Yes."

"But not as much?" she asked.

"No, not as much."

She thought about that for nearly a minute. "Maybe that's all we can ask," she finally said, then added, "at least while you are looking into your mother's murder."

"Yes," I said.

The waitress came by again, and I waved her over. She looked relieved. She took our orders with a smile. I ordered a burger and a Diet Coke.

"Did you want to order a beer?" asked Cindy when the waitress left.

"Yes," I said.

"But you didn't."

"No, not this time."

Cindy took my hands and held them in hers. "I love you, you big oaf."

"Yes, I know," I said.

9.

The morning sun was shining at an angle through the window behind me.

My feet were up on the corner of my antique desk, careful of the gold-tooled leather top. I was reading from my football scrapbook, which dated back to my high school years. The binder was thick and battered, filled with hundreds of yellowed newspaper clippings. I read some of the articles, sometimes even blushing. People can say the nicest things. I was a different man back then. Of course, I had been nothing more than a kid, but I could see it in my eyes in some of the pictures. I was arrogant, smug, and cocky. Football came easy to me. Grades came easy. Girls came easy. Life was good, one long party in those days. No wonder I missed those days to some degree. Now I've come to realize that there is more to life than football, and it has been a hard lesson to learn. In fact, I'm still learning it, every day.

As usual, I closed the scrapbook just before I got to the last game of my senior season at UCLA. I knew all too well what happened in the last game. I had a grim reminder of it every time I stood.

Outside the sky was clear, a balmy sixty-four, according to my internet weather ticker. Southern California's version of a crisp fall day. *Brrr.*

I put the scrapbook back in the desk's bottom drawer, within easy reach for next time. I next brought up the internet and went immediately to eBay, and saw that my signature was now selling for two dollars and twenty-five cents. I put in a bid for two-fifty. Next I checked my email and saw one from Cindy. In it, she described in jaw-dropping detail what she was wearing beneath her pantsuit. I flagged the message for later reference.

Two hours later, when I was done goofing

around on the internet, I was ready for real work. In the Yahoo search engine I typed "Sylvester the Mummy" and up popped a half dozen articles written mostly by historians.

I didn't learn anything new. One forensic expert determined Sylvester had probably been twenty-seven at the time of his death. Officially, he had died from a single gunshot wound to the stomach. Not much there to go on.

Of the dozen or so articles, one name popped up more than once: Jarred Bloomer, official historian for the Rawhide Ghost Town Museum. He called himself the world's greatest expert on Sylvester the Mummy.

It's always nice to be good at something.

I knew from my interview with Detective Sherbet that Bloomer and his assistant were the last two people to see Willie Clarke alive. If I've learned one thing as a P.I., it's to take note when a name appears more than once in a case.

I sat back in my chair, laced my fingers behind my head. Perhaps it was time to visit Rawhide and Jarred Bloomer.

But first a little nap. Detecting was hard work.

I was dozing in that very same position when I heard a deep voice say: "Get off your lazy ass, Knighthorse. It's the middle of the day."

I knew that rumbling baritone anywhere, for I hear it in my dreams and sometimes even in my nightmares.

Standing before me was Coach Samson, my old high school football coach.

10.

From his oversized calves to his bright green nylon coach's jacket he always wore, Coach Samson exuded coachness. He filled the client chair to its capacity, as he did all chairs unfortunate enough to cross paths with his profuse posterior. His skin was a black so deep it sometimes appeared purple. Then again I'm color blind, so what did I know?

Coach Samson looked around the office, breathing loudly through his wide nostrils. I could hear his neck scraping against the collar of his coach's jacket.

"You think pretty highly of yourself, Knighthorse." His voice was gritty and guttural. It came from deep within his barrel chest, able to reach across football fields and high into stadiums.

"No, sir. I mean, yes, sir. Those were good memories. If you look hard enough at the picture over my right shoulder, the one with two bullet holes in it—don't ask—you can even see yourself."

He leaned forward, squinting. "All I see is someone's belly."

"Yes, sir. Your belly."

He shook his head, and continued his slow inspection of the office. "What happened with the offer from the San Diego Chargers?"

I knew that question was coming. I had spent last summer preparing for a return to football, strengthening my injured leg, only to realize the passion to play was gone.

"I decided football had passed me by."

His gaze leveled on me. I shifted uncomfortably. "You could have made their squad, Knighthorse. They were desperate for a fullback. Hell, they still are."

"I'm a good detective."

"Any idea what the minimum salary is in the NFL?"

"Probably a little more than my fee."

"What is your fee?"

I told him.

He grunted. "People actually pay you those fees?"

"Lots of people out there want answers. I give them answers."

He shifted in the seat. The chair creaked. If the subject wasn't football, Coach Samson grew uncomfortable. "So it wasn't about the money."

"No."

"Then what's it about?"

"I have a life here. I'm good at what I do. I'm a different man than when I was twenty-two."

We were silent. I wondered why he was here.

"Do you miss football?" he asked.

"Yes and no. I don't miss the pain."

"You want to come back?"

There it was.

"Depends in what capacity."

"How about the capacity as my assistant coach. The team has fallen on hard times. We're halfway through the season and we need a spark."

"You think I can be the spark?"

He leveled his hazel eyes on me. "Stranger things have happened," he said. "It's not full time, Jim. I know you're busy with...whatever the hell it is you do here. Show up when you can, once, twice a week. Be there for the games Friday nights." He paused, looked down. "I have no money for you, though. Strictly volunteer."

Inglewood High barely had enough to pay his salary.

I didn't have to think about it. "Would be an honor."

"Practices start at two. Don't be late."

"Wouldn't dream of it, sir."

11.

Sanchez and I were at the 24-Hour Fitness in Newport Beach. I liked going there because they were always open, except Friday and Saturday nights, in which they closed at 10 p.m.

"You see," I was saying, as we were doing dumbbell lunges, "they're only open twenty-four hours a day five days a week."

Sanchez said, "Will you give it a rest."

I set the dumbbells down. We were using sixty-pound weights. Sanchez picked them up and began his set, lunging his ass off.

I said, "Should be something like: 24-Hour Fitness Some Days, 6 a.m.-10 p.m. Other Days."

"Catchy," said Sanchez.

"But accurate."

"Not all 24-Hour Fitness close early on the weekends," he said. "And not all of them close at ten, some close at eleven."

"Then the name change should be on an establishment by establishment basis."

"That would be chaotic."

"But accurate."

Sanchez shook his head. He finished his lunges, and placed the dumbbells back on the dumbbell rack. He said, "When are we going to start using the seventies?"

"When you get strong enough for the seventies."

"Hell, I've been waiting for you."

We moved over to the squat rack, and used every available plate we could find. The bar sagged noticeably. People were now watching us. At least two of those people were handsome women.

"There are some handsome women watching us."

"I hate that phrase," said Sanchez.

"'There are some handsome women watching us'?"

"No. 'Handsome women.' Women are *beautiful*. Men are handsome."

"You think men are handsome?"

"I think I am handsome. I think you are an ugly Caucasian."

I positioned myself under the barbell and began squatting away. When finished, Sanchez helped me ease the thing back on the rack. My leg was throbbing. The steel pins holding my bones together felt as if they were on fire.

"You were gritting your teeth," said Sanchez. "Too heavy, or the old broken leg excuse?"

"The old broken leg excuse."

He stepped into the squat machine. I did some quick calculations. We were squatting with nearly five hundred pounds. Sanchez did ten reps easily.

"Besides," said Sanchez, when finished, "I am a married man with three kids. I don't care if two women are looking at us."

"Then why are you now flexing your calves?"

"Because it's a free country."

"Tell that to Danielle."

"I'd rather not."

"Thirsty?" I asked.

"Sure."

We showered, changed and ordered drinks at

the gym's juice bar. I got a Diet Pepsi and Sanchez got something called a Sherbet Bang. We sat on red vinyl stools and leaned our elbows on the metal counter while the bartender mixed the Bang. The counter was cluttered with protein mixes, protein bars and protein supplements.

"Why not just eat a steak?" said Sanchez.

"Not enough protein."

Our drinks came. From where we sat at the gym's juice bar, we had a good view into the aerobics room. At the moment, about thirty women and a handful of men were stretching, as we used to call it back in the day. Now it's called pre-aerobics.

"Jesus got jumped yesterday," Sanchez said. Jesus was his eleven-year-old boy. "Danielle and I spent the night with him in the hospital."

"You mean Jesus?" I pronounced it the Western way.

"His name is *Jesus*, asshole," said Sanchez, pronouncing it the Spanish way: *Hay-zeus asshole*.

"How's he doing?"

"Stayed home from school today. Nothing broken, although he lost a tooth."

"Who jumped him?"

"Eight or nine kids, best I can tell."

"Any reason, or was this just a friendly neighborhood random act of violence?"

I could tell Sanchez was doing all he could not to crush the Styrofoam cup in his hand. Probably didn't want Sherbet Bang all over the front of him. "Apparently, one of the gang's girlfriends took a liking to *Jesus*."

"Nothing wrong with that," I said. "We could all use a little Jesus."

Sanchez ignored me. At least I amused myself.

"*Jesus* wants revenge. That's all he talks about. Thinks he can take each of these punks. One at a time. Individually."

I nodded. Probably could. *Jesus* was a tough kid.

"And I'm going to take him around so that he can do just that, hunt these punks down. All he wants is a shot at them. One on one."

"*Mano y mano*."

"Now you're getting it," he said. "Want to come?"

Sanchez was gazing absently over at the aerobics room, but I suspected he didn't have much else on his mind other than his son. Certainly not pre-aerobics vs. stretching.

"You're asking because you want to use my car," I said.

He shrugged.

I continued, "Because you're a cop. And you

want to remain anonymous, because cops probably shouldn't be endorsing youth viol-ence."

"Something like that."

"Sounds like fun," I said. "When does the ass-kicking begin?"

"In a few weeks. We'll let him heal a little."

"Then unleash him?" I said.

Sanchez nodded.

"Like the Second Coming," I said.

"Second Coming?"

"It's a Biblical prophecy."

Sanchez rolled his eyes. "Christ," he said.

"Exactly."

12.

Cindy and I were at a trendy Thai restaurant called Thaiphoon.

"I love this place," Cindy said after we were seated next to a window overlooking a vast parking lot. "But you hate eating here."

"Hate is a strong word."

"But you come here for me."

"Yes."

I ordered a club soda, although I wanted a beer. Cindy ordered a Diet Coke, and probably only wanted a Diet Coke.

"I am so proud of you," Cindy said.

"I am too," I said.

"You don't even know what I'm talking about."

"No," I said. "I'm just proud of myself in general."

Our drinks came. Fizzing water for me; fizzing brown chemicals for her. Next, we ordered dinner. I picked something that sounded familiar and hearty.

When the waitress left, Cindy said, "I'm proud of you because I know you would rather have had a beer."

"Yes."

"But you didn't order one."

"No, not this time."

She smiled at me and there was something close to a twinkle in her eye.

"How's the mummy case coming along?" she asked.

"Today was research."

"You hate research."

"Yes, which is why I spent most of the day playing Solitaire."

Our soup arrived. Cindy dipped her over-sized plastic spoon into the steaming broth and slurped daintily. I slurped less daintily, and three spoonfuls later pushed the witch's brew aside.

"You're done already?"

"I don't want to spoil my appetite."

"This coming from a guy who eats a dozen donuts in one sitting."

"I've scaled back to a half a dozen."

She sipped another spoonful, her pinkie sticking out at a perfect ninety-degree angle.

"I still think it's an accident," said Cindy.

"But I'm not getting paid to think it's an accident."

She nodded. "You're getting paid to think 'what if'."

"Exactly," I said. "As in, 'what if' I slipped under this table and really turned up the heat in this place?"

"You would never fit under the table."

"Tables are made to be overturned."

"We would never be able to come back."

"What a shame."

"Nice try," she said. "So any thoughts on who might want the historian dead?"

"I figure someone who stands to lose if Sylvester the Mummy's identity were ascertained."

"Big word for a detective."

"I'm a big detective."

"Not sure that correlates."

"Big word for a professor."

"I get paid to use big words," said Cindy.

"The murder is over a hundred and twenty years old. The murderer is long gone. Who could possibly stand to lose?"

"Perhaps the family of the murderer. Perhaps there's a deep dark secret."

Cindy's eyes brightened the way they do when she finds me particularly brilliant. I've learned to treasure these rare moments. She was nodding her head. "Yes, a good start. Any families stand out?"

"There's one that has potential. They're called the Barrons, and they own the town of Rawhide."

"Own?"

"Yes, own. But keep in mind this isn't a real town anymore; it's a tourist attraction. Back in the 1970's the county of San Bernardino was going to level what remained of the mining town, until a man named Tafford Barron purchased it for cheap and rebuilt it into a sort of amusement park. Barron is quoted as saying he couldn't let a town built by his family be destroyed."

"Seems innocent enough."

"Sure," I said. "Now he's running for the House of Representatives. Election's in six months. According to the local paper out there, Barron has a shot of winning this thing."

Cindy was nodding and grinning and eating.

Multi-tasking at its best. "And what if this historian, Willie Whossit—"

"Clarke"

"Willie Clarke comes in and digs up some incriminating evidence."

"Or embarrassing evidence."

"Yes, embarrassing. Either way, something like this could derail a campaign."

"Possibly," I said. "It's at least a start."

Cindy was looking at me over her Diet Coke with something close to lust in her eyes.

"What?" I said.

"I like this," she said.

"You do?"

"I love talking about your cases. I love watching you sort through your case. I love being a part of the process, even if it's from the outside looking in. Being a detective might not have been your first choice in life, but you were born to do it, and I respect you so much for that."

"I was born for something else, too," I said.

"Football?"

I shook my head slowly.

"Ah," she said, blushing. "That."

13.

I am not mechanically inclined by nature. I am more of the warrior/lover/artist type. But I do know the basics of car maintenance. So before I headed out into the desert, I topped off the Mustang's water, checked the oil, tire pressure, air filter and anything else that crossed my mind. A few years back I had the engine rebuilt. Since then, the car ran smooth as hell, which was the way I preferred. More than anything, the car was paid off. A key factor to any struggling detective.

I drove north along Highway 15, the main artery into Las Vegas from southern California. Needless to say, I sat in some traffic. With some time on my hands, and being one of the few who didn't have gambling on the brain, I was able to relax and enjoy a good book on tape. The book was about things called hobbits and a very important ring.

An hour later I was in the Mojave Desert, passing through cities called Hesperia and Victorville. I wondered if there was a Jimville somewhere. And if there wasn't, there should be.

The Mojave Desert is famous for its kangaroo rats and Joshua trees. Stephen King once set a story out here, about a Cadillac. Always liked that story.

I wondered if there were any Jim trees.

The heat was intense and uncomfortable. My windows were down, my only air conditioning. Sweat soaked through the back of my shirt and was probably puddling on my leather seat. Nice.

Every now and then someone spotted my cool car and gave me a thumbs-up gesture. I accepted the gesture with a gentle nod of my head. Every now and then someone spotted the cool driver driving the cool car, and gave me a smile. As these were mostly women, I returned the smile. Cindy would have been jealous. Luckily, Cindy wasn't in the car. Smiles are not cheating. Smiles, in my book, are okay. Unless she's smiling at other men. Then it's not okay.

Hypocrite.

I headed off Highway 15 onto a much smaller, one-laned highway. I drove alone for many miles.

Luckily, I had hobbits to entertain me. Unfortunately, the little guys were in a fair bit of trouble, as there seemed to be a lot of interest in this ring.

I checked my temperature gauge. All was okay.

The road was flat, surrounded by a lot of stark, rocky protrusions that were too big for hills and too small for mountains. I racked my brain for all words associated with mountains, but could think of only crags and hillocks. I decided on *smallish mountains*.

At any rate these smallish mountains were bare and lifeless and would have been equally at home on Mars or Venus—where, as legend has it, men and women are from. Except these burning rocks weren't barren and empty. Life flourished here, to a degree. Snakes lived in holes. Kangaroo rats avoided the holes with the snakes. Plants clung to life in ways that made sense to evolutionary biologists but seemed remarkable to the rest of us.

A car was coming about a half-mile away. The first car in 20 miles. I was giddy with anticipation. A man was driving. A woman was looking down at a map spread across the dashboard. The backseat was piled with suitcases and clothing. They never saw me waving.

The hobbits escaped the clutches of some very wicked creatures. This was followed by a lot of history of a land called Middle Earth. I almost went to sleep, but persevered, and was rewarded by some more history of Middle Earth. I turned the tape off, for now.

My timing couldn't have been better.

Nearly two hours after leaving Orange County, as I crested a sort of rise in the road, Rawhide Ghost Town appeared before me.

Howdy partner.

14.

Rawhide Ghost Town was nestled in a narrow valley between high sun-baked cliffs dotted with mine shafts. Consisting mostly of shops lining a single dirt road and much smaller than its cousin up north, Calico Ghost Town, Rawhide looked more like a Western-themed strip mall.

I parked in front of the first store that grabbed my eye, Huck's Saloon. For good measure, should anyone show up on a horse, a hitching post still ran the length of the town.

Currently, no horses were hitched. Although a handful of cars and trucks were parked in front of various stores, the town appeared mostly empty, a true ghost town.

A hot wind swept down Main Street, moaning like the damned and pushing dust before it. Probably the dust was hot, too. No trees or shade. No relief from the sun unless you went inside somewhere.

So I decided to go inside somewhere, and I chose the saloon. No surprise there.

I pushed my way through a pair of swinging doors. Always wanted to do that. And not even a *squeak* after all these years....

The saloon was empty. No cowboys knocking back a few. No barroom fights in progress. No bartender cowering behind the bar because word had spread that Big Bad Jim Knighthorse was coming to town. I tipped my Anaheim Angels hat at the empty room, stuck my thumbs in my pockets, and moseyed on into the saloon.

It was a real saloon, so far as I could tell. There was even a stage for the dancing girls and a player piano on the floor beneath it. Sadly, no dancing girls. I sat at the wraparound bar. Before me was a huge mirror. There were some bottles of not-so-authentic liquor stacked in front of the mirror. I smiled at the handsome man in the mirror. He smiled back, and we played that game for perhaps another two seconds.

A woman appeared from the back of the bar, spurs jangling, carrying a case of Bud Light. She was wearing a cowboy hat, and a bright smile. I have the effect on people.

"Howdy, partner," she said.

"Howdy ma'am," I said. "Is this where I tip my hat?"

"Maybe if you were wearing a cowboy hat." She put the case into a glass refrigerator. I noticed in passing her arms were roped with muscle. "Were you waiting long?"

"Just sat down."

"Good. What can I get you?"

"Rolling Rock, no glass. And some information, no glass."

She opened the refrigerator door again, grabbed a green bottle and placed it on top of a little square napkin to protect the deeply rutted counter top. Her work done for the morning, she leaned a curved hip on the bar. Her dark hair was pulled back in a ponytail. She crossed her arms under her chest. The long sleeves of her red-checkered flannel were rolled up to her elbows. Veins crossed her forearms, just under the skin. She looked like she could kick Calamity Jane's ass.

"So what kind of information are you

looking for?" She was smiling at me. I think she thought I was cute. Stranger things have happened.

I showed her my P.I. license. She leaned forward and studied it. "Wow, a real live private investigator. In a ghost town, no less."

"Ironic, isn't it?"

"Very," she said. "Nice picture."

"My girlfriend says I look urbane and dashing."

"Girlfriend?"

"Yup."

"The good ones are always taken."

"This one is, alas."

"Knighthorse sounds Native American," she said.

"My great great grandfather was Apache."

"Hey, we could play cowboys and Indians."

"Sounds naughty," I said.

She grinned. "So what's a detective doing all the way out here?"

I told her about the case.

"Willie Clarke," she said, thinking. "The guy they found dead in the desert?"

"One in the same."

She bit her lip, frowned. Re-crossed her arms. "But I thought they ruled his death an accident."

"So they did."

"But you think different?"

"I'm being paid to think different."

"Paid by whom?"

I shook my head.

"Top secret," I said. "Did you ever meet Willie Clarke?"

"Once. He came into the bar and we chatted. He told me he was here to look into the identity of Sylvester. You know Sylvester? Wait, of course you do, you're an ace detective."

I winked and shot her a blank with my forefinger.

"Willie was a young guy," she continued, "said he was just out of college."

"What was your impression of him?"

"Smart, funny. Sort of rugged, too."

"Did he seem like the type who could take care of himself?"

She was nodding as I asked the question. Her eyes narrowed and she frowned a little. "Yeah, definitely. He didn't look like a historian."

"More manly than me?"

She winked. "Almost, but not quite."

"Did he seem the type who would get lost in the desert and run out of gas?"

"That's asking a lot, he only came in for a Diet Coke. But, if I had to answer...."

"And you do," I added.

"I would say he seemed the type to have a map on hand, but keep in mind I only met the guy for ten minutes."

"They say he ran out of gas," I said. "And I'm willing to bet he's also the type to make sure he topped off his gas before heading out into the desert. Would be stupid not to, and everyone seems to agree Willie was pretty smart."

She was nodding. "Maybe he ran out of gas while looking for a way out."

"Maybe," I said.

"But you don't think so."

"His truck was found close to the site. Which suggests he ran out shortly after leaving the others," I said. "Did the two of you talk about anything else?"

She bit her lip. "He mentioned he'd been hired to look into Sylvester's identity, and I asked if he had spoken to Jarred."

There he was again. Jarred, Rawhide's official town historian, and curator of the Rawhide Museum.

"Why?"

"Because Jarred thinks of himself as the world's greatest expert on Sylvester the Mummy."

"And had Willie?"

She nodded. "He said Jarred was being rude

and unhelpful at best. Which sounds like Jarred. He takes his work entirely too seriously. Now he's working on his magnum opus."

"Magnum opus?"

"It's the history of Rawhide. Jarred thinks it will help establish him as a serious historian. You know, make a name for him. That's pretty important to Jarred."

"And he picked Rawhide to make his name?"

She nodded, grinning. She picked up a towel and started wiping something behind the bar, below my eyesight. It was a habit all bartenders have: just wiping the hell out of things.

"He says Rawhide is untapped material. He's going to put it on the map, so to speak."

"Rawhide is on the map."

She giggled.

I finished the rest of my beer in one swallow. I wanted eleven more for an even dozen. "Thank you for your time, you've been very helpful."

"You don't want another beer?"

"Duty calls."

She looked sad. The bar was empty. I was her only entertainment. "So where you headed now?"

"Figure I might as well talk to Jarred before he goes making a name for himself and thinks he's too important to talk to me."

She grinned. "He's four stores down. The adobe building."

I tipped my hat. "Ma'am."

Luckily, the swinging doors were just as much fun going as coming.

15.

I stepped out of the saloon and onto the surface of Venus. Or close to it. Hell, I felt myself mummifying on the spot, and almost turned around for more beer.

I passed a leather shop, general store, and glass blowing shop, and soon came upon a smallish adobe building set back from the boardwalk. The sign out front read: *Rawhide Museum, Free Admission*.

Now we're talking.

I paused, listening. From somewhere nearby

I heard the sharp report of rifle shots. From my research, I knew there was a shooting range just outside of town.

Praying for air conditioning, I entered the museum.

***

My prayers were answered. Maybe I should be a priest.

Cool air blasted my face the moment I stepped into the small museum, itself nothing more than a converted frontier house, filled to overflowing with antique mining equipment. Hardhats, lanterns, pick axes, carts, stuff I didn't recognize, stuff I did but didn't know the names of. I had the general sense that mining in the days of yore took a lot of muscle, and probably a lot of nerve. Not to mention light. In one corner, a display let children pan for fool's gold. Along the walls, dozens of black and white photographs showed the town in various stages of growth and decline. Many featured hardened men sporting thick handlebar mustaches.

A door was open to my right, leading into what might have once been a bedroom, but now was an office. Inside, a smallish young man with wire rim glasses and a goatee was working furiously on a computer, pounding the keyboard with a vengeance, oblivious to me. I studied him briefly, and concluded he would have loo-ked better with a handlebar mustache.

I knocked on the door frame, and he jumped about six inches out of his seat, gasping, clutching his heart. He snapped his head around, his eyes wide behind his thick glasses.

Jumpy little fellow.

"Oops," I said. "Of course, I could say I should have knocked, but that's just what I did."

"Oh, it's not you," he said, settling back in his chair, letting out a long stream of air. The brass nameplate on his desk read: *Jarred Booker, Town Historian*. "Just lost in my writing, you know."

"Oh, I know."

"Oh, do you write?"

"No, I was just trying to be agreeable."

"I see," he said, frowning. "Anyway, I haven't had anyone step in here for...oh, a few days."

"Maybe the price scares them away," I said.

"Any freer, and I would have to pay them."

"It's an idea."

"Are you here for a tour?" he asked.

"Not exactly."

I opened my wallet and showed him my license to detect, complete with my happy mug. A small grin, no teeth. Eyes bright, but hard.

The picture was worth a thousand words, and one of them was *roguish*.

"What can I do for you, Mr. Knighthorse?"

I told him I was hired to investigate the death of Willie Clarke and that I was here to ask a few questions. Jarred stared at me for a moment, then got up and crossed the room and closed the door and went back and sat behind his desk again.

He said, "I was told not to talk to anyone about Willie Clarke."

"Told by who?"

Jarred leaned back in his chair and studied me. The glow from his monitor reflected off his glasses. So nice it reflected twice.

"Tafford Barron?" I asked. Shot in the dark.

He looked a little surprised. "Yes."

"Any idea why he doesn't want you talking to me?"

"None that I can speculate on. Besides, I've already told the police everything I know."

"Sure," I said. "I'd like to hire you to take me to the same place you took Willie Clarke."

"In the desert?"

"Yes."

"Why?"

"Part of the investigation. Scene of the crime."

"According to the police, there's been no

crime. It was an accident."

"Sure," I said. "Which is why Tafford wants to keep you from talking to me."

Jarred shrugged. "He doesn't want any more bad publicity for the town."

"Bad publicity for the town, or for his campaign?"

"I wouldn't know anything about that."

At that moment a back door to the office opened and bright sunshine flooded the narrow room. A pretty blond girl in her mid-twenties entered through the door, shut it quietly behind her, and stood blinking, letting her eyes adjust to the dim light. She wore jeans, a red cowboy shirt and boots, the Rawhide dress code. She was also holding a rifle. She didn't know I was there, at least not until her eyes adjusted.

"Best day yet, Jarred," she said. "I couldn't miss. Oh, hello."

"Howdy, ma'am." I tipped my hat. I was getting better at that.

She grinned. "Howdy."

"I'm sorry I can't help you, Mr. Knighthorse," said Jarred loudly, drawing my attention back to him. "My hands are tied."

"Tied about what?" said the girl.

"I'll tell you later," said Jarred.

"I'm investigating Willie Clarke's death," I said. I looked at Jarred. "I prefer to tell her now."

"Oh," she said, frowning. "Willie Clarke."

"You must be Patricia McGovern." I remembered her from the police report. She and Jarred had escorted Willie out into the desert together. She was the other person I wanted to talk to.

She nodded. "Yes, I'm Patricia. I'm sorry, I don't know your name."

I gave her my most winning smile. "I'm Jim Knighthorse, detective extraordinaire."

Her eyes widened. "A detective?"

"Yes, ma'am."

"Good day, Mr. Knighthorse," said Jarred, standing. "We have nothing further to add to your investigation."

I was watching Patricia. Mostly, I was observing her reaction to Jarred's unfriendliness towards me. She didn't like it. She seemed about to say something, but then bit her lip. Maybe she didn't want to lose her job, either.

So I left, but first I handed them each a business card. Patricia looked at it as if I had handed her a two-dollar bill. Jarred tried to hand his back. Instead, I left his on his desk.

I tipped my ballcap toward Patricia. She smiled tightly, and I left the office.

And Rawhide altogether.

16.

The next day I was sitting in Detective Hansen's office on the third floor of the Huntington Beach Police Station. Today Hansen was wearing dark blue slacks, a powder blue Polo shirt with a shoulder holster, and loafers with no socks. I knew this because his feet were up on the desk, ankles crossed. His perfect hair was parted down the middle. Fit and tan, he was the quintessential Huntington Beach cop.

I motioned toward his clothing. "Items A & B, page one twenty three of the Nordstrom's men catalog?"

"Close," he said. "Ordered from Macy's. Wife picked them out. Thought I should set the standards for hip and cool for Huntington Beach PD."

"Which, itself, sets the standards for hip and cool for police departments everywhere."

"Sure."

"So, if you follow that train of logic, you are the hippest and coolest cop this side of the Mississippi. Perhaps ever."

"Gimme a break, Knighthorse."

Something caught my eye. Actually two somethings. Hansen's office overlooked a big alabaster fountain. The fountain was of mostly of a nude sea nymph. A buxomly sea nymph.

"Distracting, huh?" said Hansen.

"The sea nymph?"

"Whatever the fuck it is," he said. "Why the hell did they have to make her tits so goddamn big?"

"Because they could."

"So what can I do for you, Knighthorse?"

I told him about my mother, the picture, and why I was there. As I spoke, his eyes never wavered from mine. I finished the story. Hansen continued looking at me and then started shaking his head. His perfect hair never moved.

"Shit, Knighthorse, I never knew."

"Few do."

"The case is closed?"

I nodded. "I'm re-opening it. Unofficially."

A corner of his lip raised in a sort of half smile. "Of course. And you have a picture of the perp, or the presumed perp?"

"Yes."

"And the picture's twenty years old?"

"Yes."

He sat back in his chair, ran his fingers through his hair. His fingers, amazingly, were tan. And his hair, amazingly, never moved. Only grudgingly made some space for the fingers. Otherwise held its ground. I waited. Hansen thought some more.

"Maybe we can ID him," he said.

"Mugshots?"

"We have them that far back, of course. Sound good?"

I nodded. "Sounds good."

Ten minutes later we took an elevator down to the basement. He left me alone in a dusty backroom and, surrounded by outdated computers and boxes of old case files, I looked at the faces of hundreds, perhaps even thousands of Orange County's most hardened criminals of yesteryear.

But not the face I was looking for. And as I took the elevator back up from the basement, I

was looking forward to crossing paths with the
buxomly sea nymph.

17.

With Sanchez directing me, we drove slowly through a quiet residential neighborhood filled with small suburban houses. It was late evening, about 7:00 p.m. We were about nine blocks from Disneyland. Hard to believe there was going to be a royal ass kicking down the road from the happiest place on Earth.

While we drove, Jesus walked me through it. "Charlene and I were walking home through Hill Park. It's a shortcut from school."

"I don't like you walking through Hill

Park," said Sanchez. "That park's trouble."

Jesus and I ignored Sanchez.

"Charlene is...?" I asked.

"My girlfriend. At least one of them."

"How many do you have?"

"Two, but I keep two or three on the side."

"For emergencies?" I asked.

"Something like that."

"Lord," said Sanchez.

I was watching the kid through my rearview mirror. Jesus' face was turned, staring blankly out the side window. He was so *little*. Hard to imagine the kid being so tough. But he was. Somehow.

"Okay," I said. "So you and Charlene are walking home through the park."

"When we are surrounded by twelve guys. Most are on bikes. Some on skateboards."

"Did you run?"

"No. But I told Charlene to beat it, and she did. They let her go, of course. They were after me, not her."

"Why were they after you?"

"Nothing I did, at least nothing I could help."

"One of their girls took a liking to you."

"That's what I hear. Like I can keep track."

"I know what you mean."

Sanchez shook his head, and pointed me

down a side street. I turned the steering wheel. The Mustang rolled along smoothly, the engine throbbing.

"So they surround you, what happened next?"

"I told them all to go ahead and kick my ass, but someday I was going to hunt each of them down one at a time."

"You said that?"

"Yes."

Tough kid.

"What happened next?"

"Four of them took off running."

"Because they were scared of you?"

"I suppose."

Sanchez spoke up. "They threw a rock at him, hit him in the mouth."

I looked at Sanchez. He was staring straight ahead. His jawline was rigid. A vein pulsed in his neck.

"He who is without sin," I said, "cast the first stone?"

Jesus said, "What does that mean?"

Sanchez shook his head. "Ignore him. Go on, son."

"The rock hit me in the mouth, knocked out my front tooth. Split my lips open—lips that were made for kissing."

Sanchez shook his head. "I created a

monster."

"So I charged the one who threw it. Kid named Doyle. Jumped on top of him and started wailing on him. After that, things are just a big blur of fists and feet and blood."

"They knocked him out," said Sanchez. "His girl, whichever one she was, called 911. He was still unconscious when the police came. So were two of the kids."

I looked in the rearview mirror.

"Two?" I asked.

He shrugged. "I don't really remember what happened."

Jesus was sitting in the middle of the bench seat, looking out the right window. He was unconsciously poking his tongue through the gap in his incisors.

Sanchez told me to stop in front of a smallish house with no porch light on. There was a chainlink fence around the house.

"Who's this?" I asked.

"Brian. It was his girl who started this mess."

"How old is he?"

"Thirteen."

"How old are you?"

"I turn twelve next month."

"So you're eleven?"

"I'm old for my age."

"Boy are you ever. Need any help?"

He shook his head, but now he was looking eagerly toward the small dark house. I looked, too. Not much was going on. There was some faint light coming from the back of the house.

Sanchez said, "I cased the house last week. The kid came home alone around this time."

"Cased?" I asked.

"Yes."

"Don't you have murderers to find?"

"Don't start with me."

"Brian hangs out with his friends at this time," said Jesus. "They have a gang. Pick on kids in school, harass teachers. They get suspended all the time, smoke cigarettes, sometimes even dope."

"Here he comes," said Sanchez.

I looked down the street. A kid was coming towards us on a bike. Big kid. Much bigger than Jesus. And he was smoking. I could see the glowing tip of a cigarette. He passed under a streetlamp and I had a good look at his face. Wide cheekbones. Big head. The kid looked like a bully. Self-satisfied, content, mean.

He pulled up next to the chain link fence across the street.

The car door banged open behind me.

Jesus was out, running.

The boy flicked his cigarette away, stepped

off the bike, and reached for the latch on the chain link fence. And turned his head just as a small dark figure tackled him hard to the ground.

18.

I instinctively went for my door, but Sanchez put his hand on my shoulder. "No. Jesus wants to do this on his own." Sanchez was frowning. He didn't like this either.

"The other kid has him by about twenty pounds." And since these were just kids, twenty pounds was a significant advantage.

"Jesus fights big."

There was just enough leftover light from a nearby streetlight to see what was going on. Jesus had tackled the kid onto a grassy parkway.

Now they were rolling.

Dropped over a curb and into the gutter. As this was southern California, the gutter was dry.

The other kid, the bigger kid, landed on top.

Uh oh.

But Jesus promptly reached up, grabbed a handful of the kid's hair, and yanked him off to the side. The kid screamed.

I almost cheered.

Jesus, I discovered, did not fight fairly. And in street fighting—and when you are younger and smaller, that was the only way to go.

They were rolling again, out into the street.

There were no cars coming, luckily.

"Kid better not get dirty," said Sanchez, shaking his head. "We're supposed to be out getting ice cream."

"Jesus might have other things on his mind."

"It's *Hay-zeus*, dammit."

"Same thing."

"No, it's not," said Sanchez. "For one thing, it's a completely different language. And considering you date a world renowned anthropologist, you show a surprising lack of cultural and religious sensitivity."

"The word you want is ethnocentric."

"What the hell does that mean?"

"Thinking one's culture is superior to others," I said. "Most people in most cultures suffer from it. I, however, do not suffer from it."

"And I happen to disagree," said Sanchez. "You are one hell of an ethnocentric mother-fucker."

Shouts and the sound of smacking flesh reached our open windows. It was hard to tell who was doing the smacking.

"Your kid winning?" I asked.

"I can't tell, but it's a good bet. I told him not to kick his ass too bad. I didn't want his knuckles scuffed. His mother would have my head if she knew what we were doing. We're supposed to be getting ice cream."

One kid staggered to his feet, while the other lay in the middle of the street in the fetal position. Luckily, no cars were coming.

The kid on his feet was smallish. Dark hair. Good looking.

Son of a bitch, I thought. *He did it.*

Jesus surveyed the street, ignoring the moaning kid, spotted the bike. He staggered over to it, then dragged it over to a trash can by its front tire, sparks flying from where one of the peddles contacted the asphalt. He picked the bike up, and deposited it inside the trashcan, and closed the lid.

"Very thorough," I said.

Jesus staggered over, pulled open the door and collapsed inside. I could smell his sweat and something else. Maybe blood, maybe bike grease. Outside, a couple of porchlights turned on, including the one we were parked in front of.

"Let's go," said Sanchez.

"Anyone feel like ice cream?" I asked.

19.

Cindy and I were in her condo on a perfect Sunday afternoon watching football. During the fall, I don't work weekends or Monday nights. Cindy knows this about me and mostly puts up with it.

Outside, through the blinds, the sun was shining. We were wasting another perfect day. Big deal. Most days in Orange County were perfect. Besides, football is worth wasting a few perfect days over.

"So explain what that yellow line means

again? Do the players see it?"

"No," I said. I didn't mind explaining football to Cindy. I took pride in the fact that football seemed an overly complex game for the uninitiated. "The players can't see it. The yellow line is for the benefit of the fans."

"And you are quite a fan."

"Yes."

"Why?"

"Probably because I played the game. I know how difficult football is."

"I thought you said it was easy."

"No. I said football came easy to me. Playing my position, fullback, came naturally to me. However, everything else was hard. The grueling practices in one hundred-degree heat with twenty pounds of pads. Playing when hurt. Picking yourself up off the ground after you've had your bell rung."

"And pretending it didn't hurt," said Cindy.

"Yep."

"You rung a few bells in your time."

"That's how I made my living."

"Except you weren't paid."

"Alas, no."

"So why is there a yellow line?"

"It denotes the first down."

She snapped her fingers. I could almost see the light on behind her eyes. "You've told me that before."

"Yes."

"But you never sound impatient."

"No."

"Why?"

"Because I happen to like you."

Cindy's condo was cozy and immaculate. She had painted her north kitchen wall red. It looked orange to me, but I have it on good authority—Cindy's—that it was indeed red. The small kitchen had a ceramic red rooster on the fridge, and lots of country knickknacks. The rest of the house was laced with curtains. Cindy loved curtains. She even had curtains *behind* curtains. The walls were adorned with many of my own abstract paintings. She was my #1 fan.

Cindy's Pomeranian, Ginger, was sleeping on the couch between us, and looked like a little red throw pillow. I was working on a can of Diet Pepsi. Cindy was drinking herbal tea. Earlier, she had asked if I wanted some herbal tea, and I politely suggested herbal tea sucked ass. Now we were watching the Rams game, and eating one of her few original dishes, a 7-layer bean dip. Today, I counted only five layers.

"No guacamole or sour cream," she admitted. "So I added more beans."

"Did you say more beans?"

She thought about that, and groaned. "Oh, God, what have I done?"

I grinned and dug into the dip.

At halftime, Cindy said, "The vandals struck again."

I picked up the remote control and clicked off the TV and set the chips on the coffee table, and turned and looked at her.

"When?"

"Friday. Broke into my office, destroyed the place, ruined everything I owned. Pissed in the corners, defecated on my books."

"What did the campus police say?"

"They're looking into it. Appears to be a guy and a gal, according to the video footage they have. But both are masked."

"Any more messages?"

"I think the pile of crap on the title page of my latest textbook on world religions was message enough."

I inhaled. I was shaking. Adrenaline surged through my veins.

Cindy stroked my arm with her palm. "I'm not scared, okay? I'm used to this. I've lived with this my entire life. Many people hate my name and me. Remember, I have a permit to pack heat." She did, too. She carried a small .22 in her purse. "I can take care of myself."

"I don't want you to ever need to use your

heat."

"Which is why I have a big, strong boy-friend. Besides, you have been watching over me, right?"

"Every night you teach."

"But I don't see you."

"No," I said.

"Which means they don't either."

"Exactly."

"You are good."

"Exactly."

"Hey, we're missing the game. Looks like someone crossed over that yellow line thingy. That's a good thing, right?"

Except now, I didn't feel much like watching the game. The vandals upset Cindy, which upset me. Someone was going to pay.

J.R. RAIN

20.

It was after lunch and I was back in my office listening to my voicemail. The first message was from Bank of America. I hear from them each day. Good people. Very persistent. My pal the female computer recording asked me to please hold, followed by some static and then a human voice that said: "Hello, hello?" a few times before hanging up. I owed Bank of America many thousands of dollars. Bank of America and I were just going to have to suffer through some lean times together.

The second message was from BofA.

So was the third.

The fourth was from a man I did not at first identify. The voice was soft and hesitant. I pressed the receiver harder against my ear and replayed the message from the beginning. It was from Jarred, the Rawhide town historian, and he wanted to see me ASAP. He gave me a location and a time. I looked at my watch. I could make it if I hurried.

**

An hour and a half later, I was sipping a Diet Coke at Sol's Cafe in Hesperia. I ordered a burger and fries, and read a few pages of an emergency novel I keep in my glove box, a John Sanford I've been working on here and there.

Jarred arrived just as I was working on the last of the burger. The Rawhide historian looked a little wild-eyed and unsettled. Half of his shirt collar was turned up. He sat opposite me and looked out the window, as if making sure he hadn't been followed. Then he glanced down at my nearly finished meal.

"Been here long?" he asked.

I shrugged. "About eight or nine minutes."

"And you've already finished your meal?"

"What can I say? I'm a pig."

He gave me a half grin, but seemed distracted. He kept looking out the cafe window. I looked, too, but didn't see much, other than the nearly empty parking lot. Jarred's face was pale, the color of worm guts.

"You okay?" I asked.

"Yeah, fine. Look, sorry for the clandestine meeting." There was sweat on his brow and upper lip. The bottom rim of his glasses had collected sweat as well. Knee bouncing. Playing with his fork, flipping it over and over.

I watched all of this. "Clandestine is good. Makes me feel important." I pushed the rest of the hamburger in my mouth. "Besides, I've always been meaning to check this place out."

"Really? Oh, you're joking."

"You want a drink?" I asked.

"No, I'm fine." He looked out the window again.

"What's out there?" I asked.

His knee stopped bouncing. Wiped the sweat from his brow. "I think I was followed here."

"By who?"

"I'm not sure."

"Why do you think you were followed?"

"Because it was a Rawhide maintenance truck, and it tailed me out here."

I had seen the trucks scattered around Rawhide. "One of those blue deals," I said.

"Yes."

"Why would anyone follow you?"

He shrugged. "Maybe someone doesn't want me to meet you."

Jarred pushed his glasses up, reached inside his jacket and pulled out a folded piece of paper. He unfolded it on the table in front of me. It was a map. A hand-drawn map; of what, I couldn't be sure.

"You still want me to show you where we took Willie?"

"Yes," I said.

"Look, I was told that if I cooperated with you, I would be fired. I like my job, and I'm doing good things out there. I'm making a name for myself. Now, I can't help you directly," he said, "but this is the next best thing."

"What is it?"

"It's a map to the site."

"Where Sylvester was originally found?" I said. "And where you took Willie Clarke?"

"Yes."

I looked at the map. It seemed fairly basic, with very clear and concise directions.

"Where exactly was Willie's body found?" I asked.

Jarred pointed to an X on the map. "Somewhere along here, about five or ten miles from the site."

"Where he died of heat and fatigue and de-hydration," I said, "after his car ran out of gas."

Jarred looked positively sick. He swallowed and said, "That's what I understand. Lord, if I would have known he was out of gas, I would have given him a lift."

"You didn't wait for him?"

"His truck started right up. I thought he took an alternate route out of the desert, as he was heading back into Orange County. We thought he was fine."

"Hell of a way to go," I said. "Dying in this godforsaken heat."

Jarred looked away. That he felt guilt or some remorse for the death of the college grad-uate was evident.

"Just make sure you have a full tank," he said to me. "If you head out there."

"I will."

"And water."

"I'll stock up here in town."

"You need help with the directions?"

I looked at them again. "Seem clear en-ough."

"Can I ask you a question?"

"Sure," I said.

"Why are you going out there?"

"Scene of the crime."

"But there's been no crime, at least not

according to the police."

I grinned. "I didn't say which crime. I want to investigate where Sylvester was found as well."

"Why?"

"Because he's tied into this somehow."

"Or maybe not at all," said Jarred.

"Or not at all," I said.

"There's nothing out there, you know. It's just an empty desert valley. I've been out there dozens of times myself. It's just a big waste of time."

I shrugged. "Who knows, maybe you actually missed something."

"I doubt it. I'm very thorough."

"I bet."

He was looking out the window again, but this time he seemed lost in thought. His glasses had slipped to the tip of his narrow nose; he left them there. He flicked his gaze back to me. "Good luck and be safe." He stood suddenly. "I have to get back to work. Are you heading to the site now?"

"Sure."

He nodded and left. I watched him go. Outside, through the window, I watched him quickly cross the parking lot and get into the cab of a black Ford F-150. Before stepping in, he made a show of carefully looking around.

And then he was gone, tires kicking up dust in the gravel parking lot. He hung a right and headed east on Highway 15, back toward Rawhide.

J.R. RAIN

21.

I found a 7-11 in Hesperia and bought two gallons of water and a king-size bag of peanut M&M's. Ought to hold me. I had three-quarters of a tank of gas and decided that should be adequate. According to Jarred's map, I wasn't heading more than fifty miles out into the desert.

With the open bag of M&M's nestled in my lap, I munched away and headed east on Highway 15. As far as M&Ms go, I didn't prefer one color to the other. Colors, to me, were a moot point anyway. Still, I often wondered what the M's meant.

Twenty minutes later, I turned off Highway 15 and onto a narrow road called Burning Woman, instantly surrounded by a lot of rock and sand and heat.

I continued on and the deeper I got into the desert, the more I watched my temperature gauge. So far, so good. Hell, the bottled water was as much for my car as for me.

Occasionally, I checked my rearview mirror. No sign of a blue truck.

My windows were down. Sweat collected at the base of my spine. I sipped some water. Actually, a lot of water. The radio didn't work. So I listened to the rush of wind past my open window and to the not so gentle purr of the Mustang's rebuilt engine. There were no freeway noises out here. No honking horns or the rumble of Harleys.

This is nice.

Eerie.

But nice.

Per the map, I was to turn left onto a very small, winding road near a cluster of boulders. I soon found the boulders and made the left, using my turn signal because you never know who's waiting behind a cluster of boulders.

22.

I sat in my car and peered down into the valley. This smelled of a set up, a trap. I drummed my fingers on the steering wheel.

My car wasn't getting any cooler.

I didn't *have* to go down into the valley. I didn't *have* to observe the spot where Sylvester was found. The last place Willie was seen alive.

Sure, I didn't *have* to, but I *wanted* to. It was part of my job, part of the investigation; it was why I made the big bucks.

You could come back later with Sanchez and

check the place out first.

Or not.

I drummed my fingers some more, took in a lot of hot air. Sweat coated my skin. I stopped drumming long enough to drink some water, then resumed the drumming.

Then again, if I headed down into the canyon to look under the proverbial rock, it might be interesting to see what comes scurrying out into the light of day.

Sure, I thought, if you don't mind using yourself as bait.

A solitary hawk, or perhaps a vulture, circled the sky above, its massive wingspan forming an arching V. The sky was cloudless. The sun was almost directly overhead.

I scanned the surrounding desert; I appeared to be alone. Scraggly bushes clung to the sunbaked earth.

With my Browning tucked into my waistband, I stepped out of the car and regretted it almost instantly. The sun was unbearable, true, but it was the heat rising up from the sand that threw me off guard.

I'm getting it from both ends.

If there was indeed a sun god, he was surely smiling wolfishly down on this foolish mortal.

I brought one of the bottled waters with me, locked the car. By habit I set the alarm, and the horn beeped once, echoing down into the canyon. I think something scuttled in a nearby bush, frightened by the beep.

At least the car was safe. And I would know if anyone screwed with it.

I was wearing a tee shirt, knee-length Bermuda shorts and basketball sneakers. Boots would have been better against rattlesnakes, although boots would have looked pretty silly with Bermuda shorts. I moved the gun from the small of my back to the front pocket of my shorts, as I didn't want to sweat on it.

And headed down.

The path was steep. The rocks underfoot loose. More than once I slipped, but never fell, thanks to my cat-like reflexes.

I reached the valley floor without melting or mummifying. There, I found some shade at the base of the cliff wall where I stopped and drank some water.

The valley was far removed from anything. Why had Sly, or whoever he was, been out here in the first place?

Maybe he was lost. Maybe he was part of a bank robbing gang and this valley was their hideout; maybe his fellow bangers turned on him.

The wind picked up, bringing with it a spicy mix of juniper and sage. Or maybe I was just smelling my own cooking flesh.

I knew from my readings that Sylvester A. Myers, the man who first found Sly back in 1901, had been looking for the next great silver claim. Turns out he found a mummified man instead.

The sun angled through the narrow canyon walls. The walls were mostly dirt and sandstone, layered with the occasional swath of something darker, perhaps basalt. The hawk or vulture continued to circle slowly above. Maybe it knew something I didn't.

Something scuttled in a bush nearby.

Ah, life emerges.

Before me was a mound of three huge boulders. Screwed into one of the boulders was a very old and faded brass plaque. It read: "In memory of the Nameless who helped settle the Wild West."

That was assuming a lot. Maybe Sylvester didn't help settle anything. Hell, maybe he had done his best to *unsettle* things. Maybe that was why he was shot.

Maybe, but somehow I doubted it.

I bent down and took a handful of the hot sand, sifted it through my fingers. In my mind's eye, I saw the image of a man staggering through these canyons, gut-shot, bleeding and hurting. Alone and probably scared. Or not. Do cowboys get scared?

Yeah, probably.

To the east, high on the high cliff above, something *flashed.* Instinctively, I turned my body, narrowing myself as a target. Beside me, next to my left elbow, a section of the boulder *exploded* in a small cloud of dust, pelting me with rock fragments. I dove, rolling.

The report from a rifle followed, echoing throughout the valley.

It kept echoing even as I kept rolling.

23.

I rolled to the relative safety of the boulders, dirt and sand going up my shorts and into places it had no business going.

Worry about sand in your craw later.
Good idea.

The rocks gave some shelter, but not as much as I would have liked as I was forced to stay low to the ground with my face pressed against the hot earth. I removed my Browning, hoping sand hadn't gotten lodged in the barrel.

A second shot *thunked* near my shoes. I

jerked my exposed legs in closer as an earsplitting echo followed the shot.

Jesus, that was close.

Blindly, I eased my arm around the boulder, let loose with two shots of my own in the general proximity of the spot I had seen the reflection. The two shots were to give the shooter something to think about. I had seven more to be more careful with.

My return fire seemed to work. The shooting from above stopped, at least for the time being. I lay there behind the boulder, trying to make myself as small as possible—a difficult task at best—alert for any sounds or movement.

And then I saw movement, but not the kind I expected.

Ten feet away, emerging from the shadows of a smaller boulder, probably awakened by the gunshots—that is, if they even slept—was a tarantula. From my perspective, with my face pressed against the hot sand, the thing looked gargantuan.

The gargantuan tarantula took a few steps in my direction.

Jesus.

My skin crawled, and if I wasn't currently under gunfire attack I might have jumped up and ran.

It continued toward me. Slowly, deliberately....

I swallowed. Sweat rolled from my temple and into my right eye, momentarily blurring the little monster. When my vision cleared, I saw that it had stopped. Now, slowly, it raised its two hairy front legs up into the air. Like a referee signaling a touchdown.

More movement behind it—

You've got to be kidding me.

Issuing out of a hole at the base of the boulder, as if straight from Hell, were dozens and dozens of tarantulas. All huge. All hairy, and all moving purposely toward me, like something out of a horror movie.

Like something out of a horror movie?

Hell, this *was* a horror movie.

Suddenly the water bottle next to me exploded, spraying me with water and briefly confusing the spiders. I had actually forgotten about the gunfight. Hell, the gunfight was almost a welcome distraction at this point.

I took a deep breath, tried to focus. They were just spiders, right? Were tarantulas even poisonous? I think some were. How about California desert tarantulas? And since when did California have tarantulas?

Another shot. As the bullet ricocheted off the boulder near my head, something touched my hand. I jerked my hand away just as a particularly fat and hairy spider tumbled onto its back, its legs kicking at the air furiously.

Sweet Jesus.

I gathered myself, mentally considered my choices, realized I didn't have many, and then did the only thing I could think of. I fired a single shot from around the boulder. The blast sent the tarantulas scurrying—and me scurrying, too.

I stood suddenly, fired two more shots up into the cliff, and dashed off toward the north cliff wall. A single shot exploded in the sand near my feet. I had surprised the shooter. Hell, I had surprised myself.

Breathing hard, sweating even harder, I pulled up next to the curving cliff face, partially out of the shooter's line of fire. Still, he was somewhere above me.

At least, I *thought* he was a he.

Typical male bias.

My skin was still crawling. I think I was going to have the heebie-jeebies for a week, if I survived that long.

A jutting rock buttress partially shielded me from the sun and, hopefully, from the shooter. I waited there another ten minutes without incident. Incident being, of course, gunshots and tarantulas. Now there's a band name for you.

Keeping to the shadows of the cliff trail, I

slowly worked my way back up the steep face. Already, I was regretting not having the water.

There were no more gunshots.

Or giant, hairy bugs.

I was about halfway up the cliff face when I heard it: the sudden roar of an engine. Recklessly, I pocketed my pistol, scrambled up the rest of the way as fast as I could.

Just as I crested the cliff ridge, I saw a blue Rawhide truck hauling ass out of here, kicking up about a mile's worth of dust in its wake.

I looked over at my car; it appeared unmolested. Hopefully, it still had some gas.

A moment later, sitting in the hot seat, I slipped the key into the ignition. Praying hard, I turned the key. The engine started with a roar. I still had more than half a tank.

Thank God.

J.R. RAIN

24.

My mother's cemetery, late.

I had been drinking all evening. Cindy was away in Santa Barbara with some girlfriends. Not a bad idea since I tended to spend the weekends watching football.

Alone for the weekend, I was free to drink. Whoopee. Only I didn't want to get so drunk that I couldn't enjoy football. That would just be stupid.

Fuck football.

Okay, now I *knew* I was drunk.

With the engine still running, I was parked along Vicente Street, next to the cemetery's entrance. My lights were off.

The cemetery was massive and rolling, covering many dozens of acres. Lots of dead bodies here. Of those bodies, I wondered how many had been murdered. And of those murders, I wondered how many went unsolved?

At least one, I thought.

Would be an interesting, if not macabre, poll.

It was after hours. The cemetery was black and empty. Through the low wrought-iron fence, I could see the gentle sweep of the landscape, which was populated with black oak trees. There were no tombstones in this cemetery; rather, brass nameplates embedded in the grass. Those who cared did not allow the grass to overgrow the nameplate. I was one of those who cared.

I wondered if ghosts haunted the cemetery. If so, I wondered how many were now watching the Mustang and the drunken man inside and if they remembered what it was like to get drunk. I wondered if I really believed in ghosts.

On this night, with the full moon shining overhead, with too much alcohol coursing through my veins, it was easy to believe in ghosts.

I drank from a warm can of beer nestled

between my legs. The beer tasted horrible.

The glass inside my car was steaming over. My leather seats were cold to the touch. I was sweating, could feel it collecting above my brow. Soon it would roll down my cheeks and nose. I always sweat when I drink too much. Not sure why. Maybe it excites me.

I finished the beer and crumpled it in my hand. I picked up the bouquet of flowers from the seat next to me and stepped out of the Mustang. The cool night air felt heavenly against my hot skin. A soft breeze swept through the graveyard, rustling the branches of the many trees. That is, I hoped it was a breeze, and not some poor lost soul.

Using one hand to pivot, I jumped the low fence, kicking my legs up and over.

On the other side, I staggered down the grassy slope, crossing over the final resting places of the dead, mumbling drunken apologies, until I stopped in front of a familiar nameplate near a small oak tree.

I stared down in numbed silence.

The brass plate glistened in the residual city light.

Today was November 2nd, my mother's birthday.

There were no flowers on her grave, of course, for she had no family and no friends, other than me. I set the bouquet across the grave, in the area of her chest and her clasped hands

I closed my eyes and saw my mother as I always remembered her: beautiful and radiant, smiling warmly down at me, alive and healthy. I imagined her taking the flowers from me and kissing me on the cheek, then holding me at arm's length, cocking her head.

"Thank you, Jimmy, they're beautiful."

I opened my eyes. The cemetery was empty. The grass looked black, and my mother's nameplate was hidden now in a blur of tears. She was down there somewhere, beneath my feet. The woman who loved me with all her heart.

"Happy birthday, ma."

25.

Parents of the deceased are always difficult calls, and this one was no different. Over the phone, I explained to Edna Clarke, Willie's mother, who I was. She was confused at first, but eventually agreed to meet with me.

An hour later, I parked in front of a stylish Tudor revival in the Fullerton Hills. I turned my wheels into the curb, as any good car owner should.

At the door, I knocked firmly. As I waited, I admired the door. Cut glass, brass trim, heavy oak. Hell, my knuckles were still smarting from the firm knock.

Footsteps creaked. A murky figure appeared in the opaque glass. The deadbolt clicked, and the door swung open. An elderly woman smiled at me. She was wearing reading glasses. Behind the narrow glasses, her amplified eyes were red. I smiled back. She asked if I was Jim Knighthorse and I said the one and only. She invited me in, and in I went.

I followed her into a living room bigger than my apartment, and we sat across from each other on red leather sofas. A mohair throw rug connected the two couches. Behind me was a black Steinway piano.

"Would you like something to drink, Mr. Knighthorse?"

"No thank you, ma'am. I just have a few questions."

She nodded. Her eyes were dull. She didn't gesture. She just sat there with her hands clasped in her considerable lap. Was probably a hell of a comfortable lap.

"First off, I'm terribly sorry for your loss. I know it's difficult. I've dealt, and am still dealing with, a family loss of my own."

The dullness in her eyes faded, to be replaced by legitimate concern. "Who did you lose, dear?"

"My mother."

Her eyes watered up. "I'm so sorry, dear."

"You keep calling me dear," I said. "And I am liable to cry."

I don't know why I said that. Perhaps because she reminded me of my own mother. Or perhaps she was a mother who had lost her only son, and I was a son who had lost his only mother. We were a good match.

"You can cry, Mr. Knighthorse. I won't mind."

"Someday," I said. "I might take you up on that offer." A very fat black cat walked into the living room. Along the way he rubbed up against anything he could, and finally rubbed up against me. Good choice. I scratched him heartily behind his ears. He seemed to enjoy it, if the purring was any indication. "I understand your son lived here with you, Ms. Clarke."

"Yes."

"Did he own any credit cards?"

"Yes, but they were in my name."

"Have you received the latest credit card statement?"

She frowned a little and bit her lower lip. "No, not yet."

"Can you do me a favor, Ms. Clarke, and call the credit card company and see what charges your son made prior to his death."

She looked at me and sat for a moment, thinking. Then she got up and crossed the room and stepped through a doorway. She returned with a credit card and a cordless phone. She sat back down again and dialed the number on the back of the card. She waited, her round knees bouncing nervously. Next, Ms. Clarke punched in the credit card number.

"The last charge was at a Chevron station in Barstow," she reported. "Thirty-eight dollars."

"Enough for a full tank of gas," I said. "What day was it?"

She clicked off the phone. "The last day I saw him alive."

She was rubbing her upper arms with her hands. Tears were in her eyes. I got up from my couch and slid next to her and hugged her tightly. Her shoulders were soft but strong. She was all mother.

"But I don't understand, Mr. Knighthorse."

"Neither do I."

"Did someone make sure he ran out of gas that day? Is that what you are implying?"

I waited a moment, breathed deeply. I filled my lungs with the soft perfumed scent of her.

"Yes," I said, "that's what I'm implying."

"But the police—"

"The police are good, but they are overworked. It's not their job to look for a murder where one doesn't appear to exist. Makes for less paperwork that way."

"But you—"

"I am not the police. And it is my job to look deeper into this. And since I run my own agency, I don't believe in paperwork."

I told her about the shootout in the desert, about how someone had wanted me dead as well. How I thought the attack on me was related to her son's death. As I talked, she covered her mouth with her palm, and wept silently.

"I'm going to find answers for you," I said, "I promise."

J.R. RAIN

26.

They were waiting for us on the practice field, laughing and joking, butting heads like young rams, stretching, generally relaxing and conserving their energy for the grueling practice that was sure to come.

I approached with the other coaches through a gate in the chain link fence. Earlier, I had been introduced to the rest of the staff, and now I was wearing a maroon polo shirt, polyester shorts and a whistle. The shirts and shorts were too small. I looked like a pro basketball player from the eighties, if basketball players had shoulders like a bull. But at least I had a whistle, and sometimes that's all that matters.

As we approached, all eyes shifted to me, the new guy. *The white new guy.* The players were all wearing their generic practice jerseys, which made distinguishing them from one another nearly impossible. Yet I knew Coach Samson knew them all by shape, size and probably smell.

The team was 1-4. One win and four losses. This might be Coach Samson's first losing season in 27 years.

Unless, of course, I could do something about it.

The fall afternoon was bright—and hot. The kids were already sweating under their football pads. In heat like this, I did not miss the extra twenty pounds of equipment strapped to my back.

Coach Samson blew his whistle and the players fell in, forming seven remarkably straight rows.

I stood before the team with the other coaches. The faces behind the face masks were all black. I could feel their eyes on me. Sizing me up. Watching me, the *Whitey*. Probably wondering who the hell I was and why I was here.

They were too young to remember me.

And now they would never forget me.

Coach Samson stepped before them; his massive shadow fell across the practice field. Hell, one of the biggest shadows I'd ever seen. The others stood with their hands casually behind their backs, inspecting the integrity of the seven lines of young men.

As Coach Samson spoke, his deep voice boomed easily to the back of the columns, and no doubt to the apartments far behind the field. "The man you see before you is white, in case you haven't noticed." There were some chuckles. I smiled, too. "Despite this liability, he went on to become one of the biggest badasses I have ever had the pleasure to coach. Hell, he single-handedly filled that trophy case you see in our gymnasium."

I tried not to blush.

"This man went on to play at UCLA, and if not for one hell of a disgusting injury to his leg he would probably still be in the pros." He paused, his eyes sweeping his team. "So, can any of you tell me who this man is?"

Half the hands went up.

"Anderson."

A voice spoke up from the middle of row three. "He be Knighthorse, coach. He hold every record here."

Samson looked at me and grinned, but didn't

hold the grin too long, as that would be uncoachlike. "They know you, Knighthorse."

"As well they should."

Samson shook his head and seemed to hold back a smile of amusement. "He's here because I asked him to help us. And, brothers, we need all the help we can get. Coach Knighthorse would you like to say a few words?"

The sun angled down into my face. I'm sure my cheeks had a pinkish hue to them. I never felt whiter in my life.

I inhaled, filling my chest. Screw the speech.

"Who wants to hit the *Whitey*?" I asked them. *Hitting*, as in tackling drills, or recklessly hurling one's body into another. Reckless only if you didn't know what you were doing. And most high school football players didn't know what the hell they were doing.

Samson looked at me and raised an eyebrow. Some of the players laughed. One kid in the front said, "But you ain't wearing any pads," he said, then added, "coach."

"I graduated from pads long ago."

More laughter.

"I'll hit the Whitey," said a big kid from the back.

"Come on up," I said.

He came up and stood before me, face sweating profusely behind the facemask. Skin so dark it looked purple. A big boy, he out-weighed me by about a hundred pounds.

"I don't want to hurt you," he said.

"I promise I won't cry," I said. "Now get down in your stance."

He squatted down as sweat dribbled off the narrow bars of his facemask. He reached forward and knuckled the grass in front of him with his right hand, a classic three-point stance. Most of his weight was on his hand.

I assumed a similar position about seven feet in front of him, but my weight was more evenly distributed.

I nodded to Samson.

The coach blew his whistle.

And the kid *burst* forward, charging recklessly headfirst. With my arm and shoulder, and a lot of proper technique, I absorbed his considerable bulk and used my legs to thrust upward. He went careening off to the side. Landed hard, but unhurt.

Some gasps from the players. I think I had just brushed aside their best athlete. I helped him to his feet and patted him on his shoulder pads. He was embarrassed.

To help him save face, I said, "I got lucky."

He grinned and shook his head in what might have been amazement and went back to his place in line. I looked out at the other players. Others were smiling, laughing. Maybe, just maybe, Whitey wasn't so bad after all.

"It's mostly about technique and heart, and some skill," I said. "But you can make up for lack of skill with heart and hours in the weight room." I surveyed them. "So who wants to hit like that?"

All hands shot up.

I grinned. "So who else wants to hit the Whitey?"

The hands stayed up. Despite himself, Coach Samson threw back his head and laughed.

27.

Sanchez and I sat in my Mustang outside Harbor Junior High in Anaheim. A low vault of cobalt gray clouds hung low in the sky. We were eating donuts and drinking Diet Pepsis, the staples of surveillance. In a few minutes school would be out.

"You ever going to get a new car?" asked Sanchez, sipping his diet soda with one hand, and working on a glazed with the other.

"No."

"How about some air conditioning?"

"How much is air conditioning?"

"Eight, nine hundred bucks."

"No."

We waited some more. I think I dozed. I felt an elbow in my rib, but might have dreamt it.

"You're snoring."

I sat up. "Not anymore."

"Some detective you are."

"You're the one detecting," I said. "I'm sleeping."

"I bought the donuts, which means you're on my time."

"Fine," I said. "You have a picture of the kid?"

Sanchez removed from his shirt pocket a folded up page torn from a school yearbook. He pointed to a goofy-looking kid with big ears. "He's our man."

"What's his name?"

"Richard."

We drank some more Diet Pepsi. Occasionally, a cold wind rocked the Mustang, whistling through the cracked windows.

Sanchez dozed.

Later, I elbowed him, pointing.

Richard had emerged from the school's central hallway with a pack of kids. The pack boarded a waiting bus. We gave pursuit. Along the way, we watched Richard shove a red headed kid's face into the bus's rear window. Perhaps amplified by the glass, the freckles along his forehead were huge. Judging by the way that the redhead resigned himself to his fate, I surmised this was a daily routine.

"I really don't like this kid Richard," said Sanchez.

"Yup," I said. "Then again, the other kid is red headed."

"True."

The bus dropped Richard off, along with a half dozen other kids. We followed Richard home from a safe distance. Along the way, we watched him turn over three trashcans and knock over a "For Sale By Owner" sign in front of a house.

Sanchez said, "I ought to bust his ass for vandalism."

"You realize we're trained investigators following a twelve-year-old kid."

"Kid or no kid, he took part in a premeditated beating of a defenseless eleven-year-old. My defenseless eleven-year-old," said Sanchez. "And I'm the only trained investigator here. You're just a rent-a-dick."

"Hey, we both fell asleep."

The kid turned into an ugly white home, and promptly chased away an ugly orange cat off the wooden porch. He went inside. Sanchez pulled out a notebook and wrote something down.

"What are you doing?"

Sanchez checked his watch. "Noting the mark's time of movements, assessing the daily routine."

"Did you include abusing the redhead?"

Sanchez ignored me. When finished, he snapped the notebook shut. "Same time tomorrow, but this time we bring Jesus."

"Good," I said. "I could use some more ice cream."

28.

I was in the desert city of Barstow, otherwise known as the Great Las Vegas Rest Stop. I wasn't resting. I was actually working, sitting in front of a microfilm machine on the third floor of Barstow Junior College library.

Earlier, a rather pretty college student with hair so blond it was almost white showed me how to operate the machine. I might have flubbed my first few attempts just to be shown the process all over again.

Now, after being thoroughly trained, I

zipped through some of the oldest issues of the *Barstow Times*, currently scanning headlines in the 1880's. Barstow is an old city, and its newspaper is one of the oldest in the region. Next to me, sweating profusely, was a regular Coke. I love regular Coke, and sneak it in when the mood strikes. After driving through 100-degree weather in a vehicle with no air conditioning, the mood struck and I ran with it.

The headlines were fairly mundane. Cattle sold. Drops in silver prices. Heat waves. Oddly, no mention of terrorists, nuclear fallout, Lotto results, or presidential scandals.

I was looking beyond headlines at what would be considered the filler articles. Most historians agree that Sylvester died no later than 1880. He was found in 1901. Like a good little detective, I was going to sift through every page of every newspaper published between January 1, 1880 and December 31, 1900.

I may need some more Coke.

Most of the news was indeed about Barstow, but there was the occasional mention of neighboring Rawhide and its wealthy family, the Barrons. From all accounts, the three Barron boys were hellraisers, always in some scrap or another, constantly bailed out by their wealthy family. Fights, shootouts, drunken misconduct, and wild parties. They were the Wild West's equivalent to rock stars. Their raucous exploits often made the front page, along with pictures. I suspected I was seeing the birth of the paparazzi.

It took me two hours to go through the years 1880 and 1881. At this pace, I would be here all night. I wondered if the cute librarian would pull an all-nighter with me.

In March of 1884, I came across something interesting. One of the Barron boys, Johansson Barron, had been in a barroom fight with a silver miner. According to the article and witnesses, it wasn't much of a fight: the Barron kid stabbed the miner from behind. The miner was later treated for a superficial wound to his left shoulder, but appears to have been okay.

A week later, the very same miner disappeared.

His disappearance rallied the whole town, probably because he had had the guts to stand up to a Barron. A thorough search of all the local mines was conducted. Search parties scouted the local hills. Nothing. The miner was gone, leaving behind a wife and five children.

The miner's name was Boonie Adams.

I thought about Boonie Adams some more, then looked at my watch, in which I started thinking about lunch. I decided to get the hell out of Dodge. Or at least Barstow.

As I headed back out into the desert, with a fresh Coke nestled in my lap, I was feeling giddy. I was fairly certain I had found my man, and luckily there was one way to know for sure.

29.

It was after hours and we were with Sylvester. Jones T. Jones was chain smoking. Wet rings circled his armpits. For the ninth time, I told him to breathe and not to get his hopes up.

"This feels right," he said for the tenth time.

If I had told him that I suspected Sly was really a woman and I had proof that her name was Bertha, Jones would have said the same thing: *this feels right.*

"Well, don't get your hopes up," I said.

"Too late, they're up. Way up. Besides, I've lived my whole life with my hopes up. I'm not afraid to get them dashed every now and then. Getting your hopes dashed builds character."

"Then this might be a character-building exercise."

"So be it," he said. "I enjoy living life with my hopes up. Keeps me out of therapy and off of the mood-enhancers."

It was after eight p.m. The store was closed for the night, and most of the lights were out. I was keenly aware that I was currently being watched by about two dozen shrunken heads. Rubber, granted. But shrunken nonetheless. And I was keenly aware that I was standing in front of a very dead man. One of the deadest men I had ever seen. Hell, if I wasn't so tough, I might have been nervous.

"This store gets creepy at night, huh?" said Jones. Perhaps he was a mind reader. Or perhaps he saw me look nervously over my shoulder.

"Hadn't noticed," I said.

"We hear voices at night, you know. And sometimes we show up in the morning and the displays are knocked over."

"Maybe it's mice."

Jones wasn't listening. "Say, do you investigate the paranormal as well?"

"No."

"Too bad, I could have thrown some more work your way."

"More publicity for the store?" I asked.

"Sure," he said. Jones was shameless. "I'll do whatever it takes to get more customers in through those doors."

"Even make up ghost stories."

"If I have to," he said. "But these are real."

"Sure," I said. "Now help me move this."

And so we spent the next few minutes turning the display case away from the back wall. Soon, Jones was gasping for air, which was funny since I was the one doing all the work.

"That's good," I said.

Jones's skinny body was crowding me. I glanced at him over my shoulder.

"Sorry." He took a step back, but I could still feel his hot breath on my neck, which smelled a little like chicken wings and tobacco.

For some reason, my stomach growled.

Jones jumped. "You hear that?"

"That was my stomach," I said.

"Oh," he said, but inched closer to me anyway.

We had already moved the heavy Plexiglas case away from the wall. Ignoring Jones, I stepped around the case and examined Sly with a handy pen flashlight I kept on my key chain.

Before me, the dead man's back looked like the surface of some bizarre, distant world, complete with gullies and basins and arroyos. The splotchy skin, which looked shrink-wrapped to his bones, rippled in corrugated waves, giving the impression of perpetual motion, which was kind of ironic for a man frozen in place for all eternity.

I stepped closer, raised the flashlight up to Sly's shoulder.

My breath fogged on the glass before me. Next to me, Jones's own breath came quicker and faster. He was either going to climax or have a heart attack. I wasn't sure which would be worse.

Exposure to the elements had caused many irregularities in Sly's skin. One such irregularity was near his left shoulder blade. It was about an inch long. A tear in his mummified flesh.

No, not a tear. It was a clean cut.

An unhealed knife wound.

I stepped carefully around the display case and looked the dead man in the eyes, or what was left of his eyes.

"Howdy, Boonie," I whispered. "It's been a long time."

30.

I returned from my two-hour lunch break in time to see three men kick open my office door. Actually, one of them was doing the kicking; the other two hung back, crowding the upstairs iron railing. All were wearing stylish cowboy hats with the brims rolled into uselessness. Two of them were holding pistols.

Their backs were to me. I had been climbing the exterior stairs, coming up along the side of the building. My building is L-shaped. My office is located on the top floor in the nook of the L. They hadn't seen me, and to keep it that way, I strategically stopped climbing.

Now with the door kicked open, they looked a little confused. Maybe they thought I had been hiding inside, cowering with fear. The one doing the kicking stuck his head inside the door. He popped back out and motioned the others to follow. As they spilled into my office, I climbed the rest of the stairs two at a time and removed my pistol and entered behind them.

They were all big men, broad shouldered, wearing jeans and tee shirts. I glanced down. My doorjamb was demolished.

"Turn around and I'll shoot," I said.

They flinched, and one considered turning. I drew a bead on him. But then he thought better of it and froze. Best decision of his life.

"Good boys. Now the two goons are to bend down slowly and set their guns on my office carpet. Ignore the sorry condition of the carpet. And, yes, that's a bloodstain in the center of the room. Don't ask."

They did as they were told. And they didn't ask.

"Okay, this next part could get tricky, and really depends on how coordinated the goons are. I want them to sort of kick their guns back to me without turning."

They were both coordinated enough, kicking

back their guns with their first try, although the one on the right stumbled a bit. The guns skittered to a stop next to me, and I kicked them into the far corner of the office. Actually, considering the size of my office, the far corner really wasn't that far.

I stepped around the three men and slid into my leather chair behind my desk. I held my gun loosely in front of me.

"Everyone empty your wallets," I said.

"What?" said the third man. He was quite a bit older than the two goons. Not to mention he looked vaguely familiar. He'd recently had some plastic surgery done. His cheeks were as taut as two Samoan war drums.

"I need some cash to fix my door," I said. "Unless you would prefer I call the police?"

They started for their wallets.

"Not so fast. One at a time. You, on the left."

"Me?"

"No, my left."

"Who, me?"

"Yes, you. You first. Nice and slow."

He reached back and slowly removed a fat wallet.

"Good, now drop it on my desk."

He did so, and I went through this routine with the others. I next removed a total of two hundred and eight-two dollars. Then, using my scanner, I made copies of all three of their licenses. "For my records," I said, grinning.

I tossed back the wallets and studied the photocopied licenses before me. The two young thugs were brothers; the older man was the father.

"You're running for a House seat," I said, recognizing the name.

Tafford Barron looked sick to his stomach, sweat running down his too-smooth face. His sons' names were Jack and Bartholomew. Both were just a little older than I was, although certainly not as handsome.

"Which one's Bartholomew?" I asked.

The one on the right—my right—nodded. "I am."

"What do you think of your parents naming you Bartholomew?"

He shrugged. "Don't mind it so much."

Tafford said, "Look, can we get on with this, I have things to do today."

I looked at the older Barron. "Like putting together a campaign to run for Congress?" I asked. "Or more breaking and entering?"

"We weren't going to hurt you," he said, shrugging. "We just wanted to talk."

"So talk," I said.

"We want you to back off the case," he said sheepishly. "Of course, it was supposed to sound a little more menacing than that."

"I'm hard to menace," I said.

"I gather that."

"So why should I back off this case?"

"You mind if I sit?" he asked.

"I mind."

He inhaled and continued standing. "Because I'll pay you ten grand to drop the case."

"Does that come out of your election fund?"

"Look, pal, this is serious business, and I don't want you sticking your nose where it doesn't belong."

"I make a decent living sticking my nose where it doesn't belong."

"Decent? Look at this dump. Take the money and get yourself a respectable office." He paused. His too-tight face was flushed with heat.

"Will you also include a cowboy hat like yours?"

He blinked. "Sure."

"And the name of your plastic surgeon. He's done a marvelous job."

He inhaled. "Will you take the money and go away?"

"No."

He was furious. Tafford was used to having his way. His sons were agitated, shifting from foot to foot. They were used to their father having his way.

"Taff, did you have one of your boys ambush me in the desert a week ago?"

"No," he said. "I don't need any more dead bodies in my town, and I certainly don't need any more bad publicity."

Strangely, I believed him. Didn't seem his style to set me up in the desert, or to ambush me. He was more of the in-your-face, you've-been-warned type.

"Of course, getting arrested for breaking and entering wouldn't help my public image much."

"No," I said.

"Pretty stupid, in fact," he said.

"Yep," I said.

"Christ, what was I thinking?"

"You weren't."

"We just wanted to scare you."

"I'm terrified."

He shifted where he stood and looked at his open palms. He looked like a man waking from a bad nightmare. His two sons hadn't stopped staring at me. Perhaps they were soaking in what a real man should look like.

I said, "Taff, this mess isn't going to go away by paying me off. Someone killed Willie Clarke, and someone tried to kill me. You have a killer loose in your town."

Now he looked just plain sick. I almost

shoved my trashcan over to him in case he was going to lose his lunch.

"Tell you what," he said. "You find the killer and I'll give you the money."

"Sounds like a job," I said.

"Consider it one."

"When it's over, I'll send you a bill."

Tafford nodded. "Can we go now?"

"Yes," I said.

And they did, although I kept their money. Consider it a retainer.

31.

Across the hallway from Cindy's lecture hall was a classroom that was rarely, if ever, used. Best of all it was rarely, if ever, locked. It was furnished with a dozen or so of those wraparound desks with attached plastic chairs. Wraparound desks and I don't get along. Mostly because they were made for people half my size.

So I positioned two of them near the classroom door, where I used one to sit and the other to prop my ankles up on. From that position, siting in near darkness, I could see down the hallway in either direction, and had a clear shot of the elevator that opened onto Cindy's floor.

It was late, almost 10 PM. My feet were up on the desk in front of me, ankles crossed, hands folded across my stomach. In the hallway next to my door, the drinking fountain gurgled. The gurgling kept me company, like an old friend. An old mentally challenged friend. I had spent the last ten minutes trying to discern the different chewing gum scents wafting up from under the desk, when the elevator chimed open.

A heavy-set, middle-aged woman stepped out, blinking rapidly and peering around. Unremarkable, if not for the fact she was wearing a heavy coat, as this wasn't exactly heavy coat weather. Hell, this wasn't exactly heavy coat country. Sensing a clue, I watched her closely.

She came hesitantly toward me. Or, at least, towards my part of the hallway. She had short black hair, perfectly trimmed bangs, and thick eyebrows that needed to be plucked or weedwhacked. She stopped in front of me, her back to me, and gazed up at Cindy's lecture hall doors as if they were the gates to Heaven.

There was a slight hump in her upper spine, and I wondered if the Humanities building here at UCI had a bell tower. Then again, maybe she was carrying something heavy inside her coat.

The hallway was silent. The fountain gurgled. I could hear her breathing through her nose, saw her shoulders rise and fall with each breath.

And then, amazingly, she turned. I have no idea why. Maybe she heard me breathe. Maybe she sensed my overwhelming *manliness*. Maybe she had eyes in the back of her head.

Either way, she turned and looked right at me. We stared at each other. Her nose was a little wide, complete with a mini hump. Chin absent. Certainly not beautiful, but neither was she unattractive. I judged her age to be about forty. Didn't look much like a student, but she certainly could have been. In the least, she looked like she was up to something.

"Hello," I said.

Her mouth dropped open. Her tongue spilled out over her lower teeth like a pink tide. And then she was moving. Quickly. Back to the elevator. There, she punched the button hard enough to have hurt her hand. The elevator, which hadn't gone anywhere, opened right up. She turned her face away from me as the door closed around her.

I would remember that face. Especially those eyebrows.

When she was gone, I eased my feet off the desktop and onto the floor. I stood and moved over to the bank of classroom windows. From there, I had a clear shot of the main entrance to the building below.

I waited.

My breath fogged on the window before me. I resisted the urge to write: *I Heart Cindy.*

The door opened below, yellow light spilling out. A male student exited, followed immediately by Bushy Brows.

A tall man met her outside. He came out of the shadows of the building and the two argued for a bit, and then left together. They headed down a side trail that led to the Staff parking lot, where Cindy kept her Jetta. I watched them go until they blurred into oblivion.

I think I just met her two stalkers.

32.

Cindy was attending to a throng of admiring students. I waited in the back of the lecture hall and watched her. She spotted me and beamed me a full wattage smile that sent my heart racing.

When the last of the student groupies had dispersed, I made my way down to her desk and set a polished red apple on the corner of her desk. Cindy, who had been hastily shoving books and scraps of paper into her oversized handbag, paused and looked at the red delicious.

"Is that for me?"

"Call it a school boy crush."

Tonight Cindy's hair was pulled back in a ponytail. She knew I liked her in a ponytail. She crammed the last of her junk into her bag and walked around the desk, looked around her room, saw that we were alone, and kissed me full on the lips.

"Mrs. Franks never did that," I said.

"Who's Mrs. Franks?"

"My fifth grade teacher."

"You had a crush on her, too."

"Yes," I said. "May I carry your oversized handbag?"

"Would be a shame to waste all those muscles."

Outside, I draped my free arm over her small shoulders. Because I was a foot taller than she was, holding hands was difficult. She was, however, the perfect height for hugging, and so we worked with nature rather than against it.

"Have you ever noticed that you were naturally selected to be the perfect height for me to hug?" I asked.

She nodded. "I'm nearly certain that's what nature intended when I grew to be five foot five, on the off chance of meeting you someday."

"Nature works in mysterious ways."

"The *Lord* works in mysterious ways."

"A Darwin quoting the Bible." I said. "What is the world coming to?"

We were walking through a verdant, tree-filled section of the campus the students called Middle Earth, although I had yet to see a hobbit. Beyond, the sun had set, although the sky was still alight with its passing. Our smog-enhanced sunsets, with their pinks and oranges and purples, are out of this world.

Along the way to my car, I described my encounter with the bushy-browed woman. Cindy, amazingly, knew of her, flunking her last semester.

"You think she could be one of the vandals?"

I shrugged. "No way to know. Tell me more about her."

Cindy frowned. "Well, she was an older student, very opinionated. Outspoken Christian. Seemed to take it as a personal affront that my great grandfather was the evil Charles Darwin."

"For some, akin to Hitler."

"I'll buy that, at least on the hate-o-meter."

Now we were driving west along University Way, wending our way between stately trees, behind which were dormitories. The Mustang's windows were down. The evening air was laced with a 50/50 mixture of nature and exhaust, which, out here, is a pretty healthy percentage. Cindy looked good in my car. Her brown eyes were watching me drive. She often watched me while driving. I think she might have thought I was cute. With her ponytail, and in the old Mustang, we could have been two teens back in the sixties out getting milkshakes.

"She ever threaten you?" I asked.

"Never."

"Why did she flunk?"

"Failed every test."

"On purpose?"

"Hard to say," said Cindy.

"If so, maybe by failing the tests, she was refusing to allow a Darwin to influence her thinking. Thus keeping her spirit pure."

"I think you might be right."

There was something in her voice. I glanced at Cindy. There were tears in her eyes.

"You okay?" I asked.

"You don't think I'm the devil do you?" she asked.

Cindy was a rational person. Intelligent, maybe even brilliant. Athletic and beautiful. And she was a Darwin. But she was a person with feelings, and she was hurting.

"Only in the bedroom," I said.

She laughed and I pulled her over on the bench seat, stretching the seatbelt to the max.

She put her head on my shoulder, and I took my little Darwin to dinner.

J.R. RAIN

33.

On a chilly Tuesday morning, with the sun hidden behind patchy fog, I parked in front of a single story house in Buena Park, near Knott's Berry Farm. It was seven in the morning, earlier than I am accustomed to working, but sometimes I don't make the hours. On the seat next to me were two ventis, which, when translated from Starbucks to English, means two large coffees. Lots of cream and sugar for me, of course.

Retired Los Angeles Police Department homicide detective Bert Tomlinson was waiting on the cement porch, sitting in a wicker chair. Twenty years ago, he had been the original homicide detective assigned to my mother's murder.

As I approached, he smiled warmly, stood and shook my hand.

"Right on time, kid," he said. He checked his watch. "I head out to yoga in thirty minutes, and after that my day's booked with grandkids. And yes, I am the oldest one in yoga."

"You look younger than me," I said.

He laughed. "I'll accept fifty, but certainly not thirty-ish."

I wasn't too sure about that. The man seemed to defy the aging process, and should probably write a book on how he did it. Bert's face was line free, despite the fact that I knew he was over sixty. He weighed maybe a buck fifty, but looked strong enough to pull a people-powered rickshaw.

I handed him the coffee. "Almond mocha easy on the cream, large. As requested."

He sniffed the container. "My one and only guilty pleasure."

"I have too many to count. Oreos being high on my list."

"I refuse to acknowledge the existence of Oreos. It's easier for me that way. As far as I'm concerned, Oreos and Nabisco went belly up."

"What about the Oreos you see in stores?"

"As far as I'm concerned the bags are empty."

"You have a vivid imagination," I said.

"Comes from being a homicide investigator. You think like the killer. Some you even think like the victim. Both of which can steadily drive a man crazy."

"I do the same thing," I said, sipping from my coffee. "When I look for a missing cat, I try to think like a missing cat."

He chuckled. "You live in Huntington Beach?"

"Yes."

"My boy lives there with his family. Owns and operates the Huntington Beach Surf Museum. He'll be here any minute with his three kids. We get them every Tuesday and Thursday."

I heard noises from within the house, the creaking of floorboards, the bang of pots and pans. The neighborhood was nice, but not great. Above the rooftops, rising up like the mother of all phallic symbols, was the Knott's Parachute Ride. At the moment there was no one parachuting. The park opened later.

"I remember you," said Bert. He spoke softly. I had the impression he had once shouted a lot in his life, and now he was making up for it. "You were just a kid. Although granted you were the size of most adults. Anyway, I would never forget your mother. I followed your career here and there in the papers. You did well in high school and even better in college. You were one of the best."

That meant a lot to me, coming from a man who had left a lasting impression on me. We shared one experience: we both had seen my mother's body that night. And after his investigation, Bert knew more about my mother than any other living soul on this earth. Probably even more than my father, who was a grade-A asshole.

We were silent. Bert sipped his coffee. A car drove slowly by. In the car, a woman was talking animatedly on a cell phone, and, I think, putting on make-up. Yikes.

The screen door opened behind us, and a slender older woman came out, carrying a tray of homemade cinnamon rolls. She left the tray on a potholder and smiled kindly down at me. She patted me on the face and went back into the house.

"Even Gerda remembers you, kid. Anyway, she made these for you. They're lowfat, made with applesauce instead of oil, and Splenda, instead of sugar."

"Um, sounds good," I said.

He grinned. "Try one

I did. At least it was hot.

"Very good," I lied. "Please thank Mrs. Tomlinson."

"I will," he said. "So you are a detective now."

"Yes. Perhaps it was inevitable."

"How's that working out?"

I shrugged. The cold from the concrete porch was seeping up through my jeans, numbing my buttocks. "It's still a new agency. I like what I do. I seem to be good at it."

"You've got the instincts, then."

"I suppose."

"So you waited before looking into your mother's murder."

I nodded. "I wanted to know what I was doing before I looked into it. Didn't want to screw things up. Just wasn't ready yet, I suppose."

"So do you know what you're doing now?"

"Yes."

I took a deep breath and told him about the day my father arrived with the pictures. Bert listened without comment, sipping from his coffee, which he cradled in both hands.

When I finished, Bert frowned. "I know about your parent's last day. Went over it in some detail with your father. However, he never mentioned the pictures."

"My father had them developed and forgot about them."

Bert set his coffee cup down, put his elbows on his knees and steepled his fingers in front of his face. He contemplated his steepled fingers.

"Your father admitted to having numerous affairs. Would have been high on our suspect list had he not been out with you at the time of her death. Excuse me if I offend, but I didn't like him. There was always something different about your dad, something off. Something cold and calculating. Everything added up to him being the killer."

"Except for the fact that he was with me."

Bert nodded. "Except for that."

I took in a deep breath, filling my lungs to their max, and just held it. How could my father keep those pictures from me? How could he not care? My father, I knew, was a different sort of killer. He had been a sniper in the military, with many confirmed kills to his credit. A hair's breadth away from being a sociopath, he held little regard for things living, and even less regard for things dead. In my opinion, he was a hell of a dangerous man to have loose in our streets. But there he was, out in LA, running one of the biggest detective firms in the city, and making a shit load of money at it, as well.

Bert was no slouch. "Obviously something

was in the pictures."

"Yes," I said.

"Tell me about them."

I described them in detail, especially the three photographs of the young man.

Bert was looking at me. "Sounds like he took an interest in your mother."

"Yes."

"It's not much," said Bert. "But it's something."

"Yes."

"Any idea who the young man is?"

"No, but I will."

"The picture's twenty years old. Might be hard to find him."

"For a lesser human being maybe," I said.

"But not you."

"Nope."

"You're going to bring her killer to justice if you find him?"

"No. I'm going to kill him the same way he killed my mother."

"Slit his throat?"

"From ear to ear."

"I'll pretend I didn't hear that."

"Good."

He looked at me from over his steaming cup of joe. "I did my best to find him," he said.

"I know," I said. "I read the police report.

You worked your ass off."

"There were no leads. No clues. Forensics was in its early stages back then. Your mother had no enemies, and no friends for that matter. Your father had no motive for wanting her dead by hiring a killer—hell, they were even working on their relationship at the time of her death. She left behind no money. She wasn't seeing anybody on the side. She wasn't pregnant. From all accounts, she was a sweet woman."

"She was beautiful," I said. "She had that."

"Yes, she was."

"And someone could have wanted that. Wanted her physically, and then slaughtered her when they were done with her."

"Yes," said Bert. He looked away. "It's the most likely scenario."

"A random rape and murder," I said.

Bert Tomlinson nodded. He looked at me again and set his big hand on my knee. He inhaled deeply and patted me once.

"Go find him, son. Find him for me, too."

A black SUV pulled in behind my Mustang. Like a prison break, three young children spilled out of the back seat and up the walkway and into their grandfather's arms. Bert laughed and fell back as the children swarmed over him like a litter of puppies.

"Who are you kids?" he asked, chuckling,

completely succumbing to the unconditional love.

"Your grandkids!" they all chimed in at once. Now they were trying to tickle him. There were two girls and one boy. All were within a few years apart. The girls, I think, were twins.

"It's like this every time," said a male voice in front of me. "They love him more than anyone on the face of the earth. Definitely more than me."

I looked up. The middle-age man in front of me was handsome. Tan and in good shape. Blond and blue-eyed. He gave me a winning smile, full of white teeth. His face was weathered and he looked a little older than he was, probably due to the fact he spent a lot of time in the sun, which was easy to do in Huntington Beach. He looked familiar, but I couldn't place him. I stood. He held out his hand and I shook it.

"Gary Tomlinson," he said, introducing himself.

"Jim Knighthorse."

He held my gaze a moment, and then nodded. "Nice to meet you, Mr. Knighthorse." He turned to his father, who was buried somewhere under all the grandchildren. "I have to get running, dad. I'll see you tonight."

Bert raised a hand and waved. "See you,

son."

Gary left, and I wasn't too far behind. Bert waved to me from the porch even while his grandson swung from his arm.

34.

The morning haze hadn't yet burned off, and the sun was still hiding up there, somewhere. I considered getting some donuts, but didn't want to overdo it, as I had already had breakfast and something that resembled a cinnamon roll.

At least it was made with love.

I passed a donut shop. Then another. I came upon a third.

My willpower shattered, I hung a U-turn and made my way back to the third donut shop, and left a few minutes later with a half dozen bars and cakes and crullers, two-thirds of which were chocolate. To wash them down, I got some chocolate milk. Chocolate may or may not be an aphrodisiac, but it sure as hell was a Jim Knighthorse picker-upper. I was giddy with anticipation.

I paid two bucks and parked in the public parking near the pier. I could have easily parked in my parking space under my apartment building and walked across the street and saved myself a fistful of dollars. But what the hell, I was feeling wasteful. I ate my first donut.

The beach was mostly quiet, although the faithful surfers were out here in droves. The waves were choppy, but that didn't discourage the diehards. And in Huntington Beach, they were all diehards. I ate donut number two.

If I turned my head a little, I could see my apartment building across the street. My apartment was there on the fifth floor, overlooking Main Street. And next to my apartment, through an open sliding glass door, I could see my Indian neighbor dancing in his living room. Jaboor was wearing only cotton briefs and was singing into a microphone, although it could have been a TV remote control. He paused in front of the glass door and shook his ass for all of Huntington Beach to see. I ate donut number three. When the ass-shaking was done, he boogied away from view.

A cool breeze blew through my cracked open windows.

I contemplated the breeze. Donut four.

Outside, I gave the last two donuts, both maple bars, to the first bum I found. He seemed genuinely pleased and started on them immediately, despite the fact that they were not chocolate. Beggars can't be choosers, after all.

I crossed over to the pier, where a handful of fishermen were fishing. Not a single woman in the bunch. Behind my Oakley wraparounds, I scanned the fishermen carefully, wondering what the blond punk would look like now.

He would be near forty. At twenty, he had looked like hundreds of other surfers. Blond, tanned, healthy, good-looking. What did he look like now? Most lifelong surfers didn't allow their bodies to go to pot. No, if he were still surfing, he would still be fit and trim. I had to assume he was still surfing. It was all I had to go on.

If so, he would still have his tan. Still have his blond hair.

And if he was a lifelong surfer, he would still live in the area, or not far from here. Hard to give this weather up, unless he moved to Mexico, like some die-hards do.

But at the time he hadn't been surfing, right?

He had been fishing. But he looked like a surfer. His hair was stained blond by salt and sun. I knew he was a surfer. But that didn't mean he was still surfing. Maybe he got married and moved to Riverside to start a family.

Still, if he were a surfer at heart, even with a job and family and a long commute, he would find a way to the waves. It's in the surfer's blood. They can't escape the siren call of the waves. It's a lifelong passion.

Well, I had 40 or 50 years left on this planet. That should be enough time to cover all the beaches.

I spent the afternoon there at the pier, searching faces behind my shades. The sun did eventually burn through the low cloud layer, and when it did, and when most of the fisherman went home, I did too. Just a hop, skip and jump away.

35.

I was parked two rows down from Cindy's Jetta with a clear view of the walkway down from the east side of campus. Without a Staff Parking permit, I was risking a ticket.

The night was young and I was hunkered low in my seat. I am six foot four, so hunkering is difficult. On the floor between my feet was a six pack of Bud Light.

I drank the first beer.

Clouds obscured the night sky. The wind was picking up, blustering through my open windows, bringing with it the metallic scent of imminent rain. Students drifted in and out of the parking lot, using it as a sort of shortcut into campus.

Like a chain smoker, I finished beer number two, started on three. Drinking in the car...not exactly a role model for today's youth.

A light drizzle began to fall, turning the dust on my windshield into a thin film of muck. The drizzle turned into something more than a drizzle, although I wasn't sure what that might be. Heavy drizzle? In southern California we don't have many words for rain. We do, however, have nine different words for *tan*.

My windshield morphed into a surreal canvas as splattering raindrops fused with parking lot lights. Living art.

Which reminded me. I hadn't painted in a while. Maybe I should. Except lately I didn't feel much like painting. Instead, I felt like getting drunk every second of every day.

I opened beer number four. Two left. I considered getting more. Really considered it, but that would mean leaving the parking lot. Leaving Cindy's car unattended. Derelict in my duties as boyfriend and bodyguard. And driving with a heavy buzz probably wasn't a great idea.

Still, another six-pack sounded good. Too good.

Shit.

I needed to find my mother's killer. I needed to catch him, and I needed to serve justice, and I needed closure. No kid should find his mother dead. No kid should have to see what I saw.

It's a wonder I'm not more fucked up.

Hell, after what I've been through, I should be allowed to drink as much as I want. Maybe I would talk to Cindy about that.

Or not.

36.

An hour after my last beer, an hour in which I spent debating getting more, I saw a shape emerge from the oak trees lining the parking lot. The shape was holding something heavy.

I sat up a little in my seat, blinking through my mild buzz, trying to focus on the stumbling figure, which, I was certain, was a small woman.

She was dressed in black and wore a wool cap. She paused momentarily behind the rounded fender of a newer-style VW Bug and waited for a student at the far end of the parking lot to move on.

Once done, she crept forward again, passing in front of my Mustang, where I had a good look at her. Dark hair pulled tightly back. Straight bangs. Eyebrows in bad need of plucking. She was carrying what appeared to be a full paint can.

Her name, I knew, was Jolene Funkmeyer.

I scanned the surrounding parking lot, looking for her male accomplice but didn't see anyone suspicious. Maybe tonight she was going solo. Taking some stalking initiative.

She kept to the shadows, as any good stalker should, and moved quickly from car to car. By my best calculations, she was heading towards Cindy's sporty red Jetta, which was parked directly beneath one of the parking lot lights.

Funkmeyer hovered at the perimeter of the light, momentarily confused. Like a vampire witnessing the sun after a long night out raising hell. Finally, mustering some inner stalking courage, she stepped forward into the light and promptly tossed the contents of the paint can across the hood of Cindy's Jetta. Bright yellow splashed everywhere, even onto some of the other cars.

Then she bent over the hood and feverishly began finger-painting. Tongue sticking out the corner of her mouth. As she did so, working her way around the hood of the Jetta, I called the campus police.

I hung up and waited. The figure in black continued writing. Her face gleamed wet in the drizzling rain. Her thighs were now covered in yellow paint. Still she wrote. Perhaps she was writing her dissertation. Her face was mostly hidden, but I could see that her hair wasn't entirely black; it was also streaked with gray.

As she wrote, she looked up occasionally to scan the parking lot. Luckily, she was alone. Or thought she was alone.

She continued her magnum opus.

I watched.

Just keep writing, darling.

Movement beyond the oak trees. I looked up. Bounding along a narrow path was a three-wheeled campus security vehicle, packed with police officers. Like a scene from the Keystone Cops. Either they were here for the vandal, or someone had lost a stray golf ball.

In an explosion of grass and twigs, the vehicle burst over a curb and into the faculty parking lot, a powerful beam swept across the hoods of the car. Like a deer caught in head-lights, Funkmeyer froze in mid-scrawl and looked up. Her mouth dropped open. Then she tried to go a couple different directions at once, finally decided on one, and dashed through a row of cars and into the night. As she ran, her hands flashed yellow. Like a beacon.

The campus police made a hard right and gave chase, cutting across a connecting swath of grass. I watched until everyone disappeared from view around the performing arts building.

I stepped out of my car and walked over to Cindy's Jetta. The woman had made quite a mess of things. I read her surprisingly neat writing:

Darwin was wrong. You live a lie. You will burn in hell.

I went back to my car, resuming my vigil.

One stalker down, one to go.

37.

Cindy and I were in bed together. Ginger the dog was lying on the comforter between us. Her little face was scant inches from my face. Her little doggie breath wasn't so little.

"She needs a doggy mint," I said.

"She doesn't have bad breath," Cindy said.

"I beg to differ."

"You've done enough begging for tonight."

"True," I said. "Still, I'm surprised you can't see the green radioactive cloud hovering over her head."

"You have a sensitive nose."

"I have a sensitive something else, too."

"Sometimes too sensitive."

"Let's change the subject."

Ginger got up and stretched, legs vibrating down into the bed. She turned two circles, lay again and burrowed her little muzzle under her front paws, sighing loudly, absently licking her front paws, eyes closed. I'm not even sure she was awake.

"Any leads on the other vandal?" she asked.

"I'm looking into it," I said. "According to the police, Jolene Funkmeyer denies having an accomplice."

"The word 'accomplice' suggests something more grandiose than vandalism."

"How about vandal buddy?"

"Better."

"Anyway," I said, "turns out Jolene has been arrested before."

"For?"

I hesitated. "Arson."

"Shit."

"Spent a year in prison."

"What did she burn?"

"An abortion clinic in Buena Park. No one hurt. The clinic had been vandalized weeks on end prior to the arson."

"So the vandalism escalates into something

more than vandalism."

I nodded again. "She was arrested with her boyfriend."

"You have his name?"

"Chad Schwendinger."

"You think he's our man?"

"A good chance," I said. "The Irvine Police checked out his last known address this afternoon. He moved out long ago. And no leads where he might be. Yet."

"Maybe he's been shacking up with his vandal girlfriend."

I shook my head. "I checked out her place this afternoon. She lives alone. Although one neighbor mentioned she had seen a middle-aged man in a BMW come by on a few occasions."

"Maybe he will want revenge for the arrest of his girlfriend."

"What he wants and what he gets are two different things."

"But you'll still watch over me just in case?"

"Like a hawk," I said.

J.R. RAIN

38.

Sanchez and I were in my car on a Sunday afternoon, parked outside the big Lutheran church on Fifth and Edinger.

"He's the last one. Name's Ricardo Gomez," said Sanchez, consulting a list of names. There were eight names on the list, seven of which were crossed off.

"You do realize we're outside a church," I said.

Sanchez wasn't listening. "Ricardo hasn't been alone in nearly a week. This might be our only chance to nail him."

"I think you've let this go to your head."

Sanchez looked at me. "Hell, this went straight to my head the day I heard my boy was in the hospital. This went straight to my head the day eight boys kicked his face in."

"Take a deep breath," I said.

He ignored me. "Besides, we're doing the neighborhood a service. My son has single-handedly broken up this so-called gang. According to his school principal, these kids have been harassing students all year, not to mention vandalizing property."

"Did the principal know what happened to your son?"

Sanchez nodded. "And he knows my son is picking them off one at a time."

"What did he say about that?"

"Hallelujah."

"That because your kid's name is Jesus?"

"Hay-zeus, asshole." Sanchez looked at his big cop watch. "Church will be out soon."

"Kid named Jesus kicking ass at church," I said. "Maybe it's the Second Coming."

There was a box of donuts balanced on the console between us. I had insisted on getting the donuts at the Von's grocery store this time, which often had better donuts than most hole-in-the-wall chains. Sanchez thought getting donuts at a grocery store was sacrilegious but he ate them anyway.

"Church is out," Sanchez reported, leaning forward eagerly. "And there he is, walking home alone." I thought Sanchez might wet his pants. He pulled out his notepad and made an entry. I leaned over his shoulder and read the entry: *11:53 AM. Sunday. Church out.*

"Don't you have murderers to catch?" I asked.

"Not on Sundays," he said. "Day of rest." Then he made another entry: *Intercept target. Next Sunday. Noon.*

"Target?" I said. "You need to get a life."

"I'll get a life after next Sunday."

"You have a sprinkle on your chin."

"Fuck you."

"Such language at church."

J.R. RAIN

39.

I met Rawhide's assistant museum curator at a coffee shop in Barstow. I was nursing a Diet Coke when Patricia McGovern arrived straight from work, wearing low heels, jeans and a red cowboy shirt.

"Would you like something to drink?" I asked her.

"Coffee would be nice."

"In a coffee shop? Surely you jest."

She smiled at that. I think she thought I was funny. Or retarded.

The waitress was older than the surrounding rock-encrusted hills, although she was sprightly and had a certain spring to her step. She took our orders. One coffee, black. One refill of Diet Pepsi, also black. Everyone at the table laughed at that one. I was on a roll.

"So what did you want to see me about?" asked Patricia, leaning forward on her elbows. She was as cute as I remembered, dark hair pulled back in a ponytail. I was flattered by the intensity of her gaze, as if I was the only person important enough to look at in the diner. I happened to agree.

"Just have a few routine questions about Willie Clarke."

Her gaze intensified. "I'm not supposed to be talking to you, Mr. Knighthorse. I could get fired."

"I know," I said. "Which is why we are meeting secretly in a coffee shop, and why I am bribing you with coffee. I promise to make this quick."

She inhaled deeply. Held it for a few seconds and then let it out. The mother of all sighs. "How can I help you?"

Our drinks came, with two complimentary biscottis. The old gal winked at us and shuffled off in a springy sort of way.

"Could you describe your first meeting with

Willie Clarke?"

She shrugged. "It was about two months ago. He just showed up out of the blue one day asking about the mummy."

"What did Jarred think of that?"

"Jarred didn't like it. Or him."

"Why?"

"I can't say for sure. I can only speculate."

"Speculate away."

"Jarred's trying to make a name for himself in Rawhide. He purposely staked out Rawhide because very little has been written on it. He calls the town an untapped vein."

"Fitting for a mining town."

"Yeah, he thinks he's pretty clever."

"So Jarred didn't exactly roll out the welcoming wagon for Willie."

"Exactly. Jarred was just plain rude. Willie was just doing his job. Which, I might add, was an impossible task. I mean, how many historians before him have looked into Sylvester's identity?"

"A million?"

She grinned. "Okay, maybe not that many, but there have been a lot."

"Maybe it takes a detective."

"Someone like you?"

"Stranger things have happened."

"I'll believe it when I see it. Anyway, Jarred

doesn't own Rawhide, and he certainly doesn't own its history. Willie had a valid reason for being here. After all, the man who now owns Sylvester hired him. And all Willie wanted was to be shown the site where Sly was originally discovered. Against Jarred's wishes, I agreed to help Willie."

"How did that sit with Jarred?"

"Oh, he was furious. But I didn't care. Willie was sweet. And harmless. I mean, he really didn't know what he was doing out here. He was barely out of graduate school. Hardly makes him a qualified historian, and certainly no threat to Jarred."

"Tell me about the trip with Willie."

She did. She met Willie in Rawhide on a Saturday morning, her day off. They were just about to head out into the desert when Jarred showed up out of the blue and insisted on joining them.

"Insisted?" I asked.

"He wouldn't have it any other way, and told me in private that he didn't know if Willie's intentions were honorable or not. What a load of crap that was." She actually snorted, which was very unbecoming of her. "Willie was nothing but sweet."

"Was Jarred jealous?"

"I don't know. If so, he never showed much

interest in me before."

"Maybe he's blind."

"Thank you, Mr. Knighthorse. But to be honest, at the time, Jarred seemed to be on something. He was jittery, excited, as if he was amped on a half dozen espressos."

"So what happened next?"

She shrugged. "Jarred insisted I go alone with him in his truck. Willie was to follow us."

"There wasn't enough room in Jarred's truck for the three of you?"

"Sure, if we all sat together. But Jarred thought Willie would be uncomfortable."

"Okay," I said. "Go on."

"We drove out to the site, with Willie following behind us in his own truck." She paused and leaned forward, leveling her considerable gaze on considerable me. "Get this: once we arrive, Jarred suddenly changes his tune. Now he couldn't be more helpful."

"What do you mean?"

"Now he's answering all of Willie's questions. Laughing, joking, having a good time."

"Why?"

"I dunno. Maybe he was finally coming around. After all, Willie was easy to like."

I thought about this. While I thought about this, I drank from my Diet Pepsi, which had been sweating profusely, condensation pooling on the Formica table.

"Did anything unusual happen?" I asked, reaching for something, anything. "Anything out of the ordinary?"

She shook her head. "Not that I can think of."

I continued reaching.

"Did Jarred ever leave the two of you for any reason?" I asked. "Was he ever alone?"

She thought about that.

"Why do you ask?"

"Because I can't think of anything else."

That seemed to satisfy her. She sipped on her coffee and suddenly started nodding. "Yes, actually. He was alone."

Bingo.

"Tell me about it."

She did. It happened just after they arrived in the desert. Willie had come prepared, of course, with bottled water and sunscreen, etc. But Jarred, apparently making a last minute decision to head out into the desert, had not. In fact, he was completely unprepared. So halfway down the trail, the town historian went back up to fetch some of Willie's water from the truck.

"Willie's water?" I said.

"That sounds funny, huh."

"Yes," I said, but ever the professional, I continued on. "And Willie gave Jarred the keys to his own truck?"

"Yes."

"Where the extra water was?"

"Yes."

"And Jarred went alone?"

"Yes."

"How long was Jarred gone?"

She thought some more. "As long as it takes to hike halfway up the trail and back down again. We were at the site by the time Jarred came back."

I had been on that same trail. In fact, I had been shot at on that same trail. Altogether, it was about a half mile straight down a narrow rocky path. I mentally calculated how much time it would take to climb halfway back up and then down again.

"Thirty minutes?"

She shrugged. "He might have been gone a little longer. Maybe forty-five minutes or more. Willie and I were nearly done examining the site by the time Jarred returned."

Fifteen minutes unexplained. Long enough to sabotage a vehicle?

I said, "And when he returns he's suddenly helpful and friendly."

"It was the strangest thing. But yeah, he's answering questions and offering information."

"Quite a change."

"Yes, I was happy to see it," she said. "Finally, he was being nice."

"So then the three of you leave in separate vehicles."

"Yes."

"Except you and Jarred made it back to Rawhide and Willie doesn't."

She sucked in some air. Tears rapidly filled the corners of her eyes. The wetness amplified her eyes and made them look bigger than they were.

"What happened?" I asked.

"I don't know." Her voice cracked. "When we left, I looked back a few times to make sure he was following us." Tears were coming freely down her face. She had caught the attention of some people in the shop. She continued, "At some point we lost him. Because when I looked again, he was gone."

"Where were you when you lost him?"

"On Burning Woman Road. We rounded a bend and suddenly he wasn't there."

Burning Woman was the single lane road that eventually connected to the I-15. A very long stretch of highway. Very long and very lonely.

She continued through her sobs. "I thought maybe he had pulled over to make a phone call, or turned around to go back to the site on his own." She shrugged. "Or maybe he knew of another way out of there. I'm not exactly sure where Burning Woman heads off to."

"So what did you do when you saw he was gone?"

"I told Jarred to go back."

"And did he?"

"No."

"Why?"

"He said Willie was fine, that he had probably gone another way home, and that we had things to do at the museum."

"I thought you said you had a day off."

She nodded. "Jarred said we had a shipment come in last night, and he wanted me to catalogue it for display later in the week."

"Hardly pressing."

"Nothing at the museum could be considered pressing."

"Did you see Willie with a cell phone?"

"No, but he had called earlier to let me know he was running a little late."

"Did he call you while driving?"

She nodded again. "He was just heading off I-15 toward Rawhide."

"Do you still have his cell number?"

She reached and opened her purse and removed her wallet, from which she removed a white business card. The cell number was hand-printed on the back of it. She handed it to me. "I know what you're thinking, Mr. Knighthorse."

"What's that?"

"If Willie had had his cell phone, why didn't he call for help."

I smiled encouragingly. *Go on*, my smile said.

She continued, "And if his cell phone had worked earlier in the desert it probably would have worked from Burning Woman, too."

I let her keep talking. She seemed to be on a roll.

"So the question is: what happened to his cell phone?"

"The million dollar question," I said.

40.

After my meeting with Patricia, I bought myself a 12-pack of Bud and checked into the Desert Moon Motel near Barstow's big outlet mall, which, coincidentally, had prices similar to regular malls.

The motel room was ordinary, although this one came with a bonus double bed and a lot of stuffy air. Now forced to make a decision, I stood in front of the double beds, thinking. Finally, with the air conditioner only managing to sputter semi-cool air, I opted for the bed closest to the window.

Once settled, I had Domino's deliver a large cheeseburger pizza. I found a college football game and drank much of the beer and eventually ate the whole pizza, tossing the empty box on the carpet between the two beds, along with the empty beer cans. Gluttony at its best. The game droned on. I drank on. Cindy called a few times and each time I tried to hide the fact that I had beer breath, until I remembered she was a hundred miles away. Still, I think she knew, although she didn't say anything.

Just watching the game was making my leg hurt. So I turned it off and limped across the room and over to the window and looked out across the black expanse of desert. The motel was on the fringes of town. I cranked open the window. A hot wind touched my sweating face. The wind was infused with sage and desert lavender and probably muskrat turds. I pulled up a chair, put my feet up on the windowsill and cracked open another beer.

I awoke the next morning in the same straight-back chair with the window open and the air conditioner chugging away, still holding a half-full can of beer.

So I finished the beer, looked at my watch. It was just before 9:00 AM. The Rawhide museum opened at 10:00. I had just enough time for a

McDonald's McGriddle!

I found Jarred's address in the Barstow phone book. He lived in a condominium off of Somerset Street, in what would be considered downtown Barstow. At half past ten, I parked across the street.

My windows were down and my shades were on. The day was blistering. Heat waves rose off my hood. There was another sausage McGriddle in the bag for the ride home. I could hardly wait. Hope it didn't spoil in the heat. A chance I was willing to take.

I stepped out into the heat, opened my trunk and returned to my front seat with a plastic case. From the case, I lifted out what locksmiths call a pick gun. Next, I pulled on some latex gloves.

With the pick gun in hand, I got out of the car again and crossed the street. The sidewalks were empty. People were at work or indoors with their AC's running.

On the bottom floor, I found the unit I was looking for and knocked.

I listened, my senses alive and crackling. I could have heard a desert muskrat scratch its balls.

Nothing. No desert muskrats and no yipping dog, either.

Good.

Nowadays, pick guns are the way to go for

any locksmith. They operate on the laws of physics: action verses reaction, using the transfer of energy to compromise most locks. At the door, I slipped a slim needle into the keyhole and pulled the pick gun trigger, releasing the internal hammer, which caused the needle to snap upward, throwing the top pins away from the bottom pins. Now I adjusted the thumbwheel, then the tension wrench—and heard a satisfying *click*.

I turned the doorknob and stepped inside.

41.

The condo was stifling, and very still, which led me to believe it was empty. I clicked the door shut behind me, turned, and found myself standing in the living room. A massive mahogany entertainment center was to my immediate right. There was an old couch in front of me, and the kitchen was to my left. Sweat immediately trickled down my sides. The air was thick and hard to breathe. I considered opening the freezer door and sticking my head inside.

Nervous   excitement   fluttered   in   my

stomach. I wasn't entirely sure what I was look-ing for, but finding Willie's cell phone would be a start.

The living room was cluttered with fast food wrappers. Hell, there were fast food wrappers on top of fast food wrappers. In New York, rats would have had a field day in here. But out here in the desert, the remains of his meals had gone to a regiment of ants.

I stepped over the trail of ants and headed to the first bedroom. The room itself was a disas-ter, clothes everywhere. Ironically, the hamper was empty. Jarred must have been a lousy shot. The bed was so unmade it appeared to have never been made. Three of the five drawers in his dresser were empty. The other two were full of socks and boxers. I looked under the bed. More clothes.

Next was the adjoining bathroom. The light and fan were both still on, and the air was thick with mildew, despite the fan. Water pooled in the center of the bathroom floor. Five or six colognes lined the cabinet below the mirror; three of them toppled over on their sides. The lower half of the mirror was filmy with dried water spots. Shaving scum lined the sink bowl. On the other side of the mirror was a rusted fin-gernail clipper, Band-aides and wrinkle cream. Maybe it was a man's wrinkle cream.

The second bedroom was used as an office, and apparently it was Jarred's Holy of Holies. Utterly immaculate. Hell, it even looked freshly vacuumed. His computer was on a desk in one corner of the room. I considered going through his computer files, but doubted I would find the cell phone there. Piles of research books were stacked next to his printer, along with dozens of manila folders. A trashcan next to the desk was filled to overflowing with wadded paper. I unwadded a few. These appeared to be false starts to the history he was writing on Rawhide. From what I could tell, he had a fair command of the English language, although he used too many commas for my taste. I opened the cupboard above his computer desk. It was mostly empty, other than a small pile of blank CD-ROMs ready to be burned.

I left the study and went back through the kitchen and out through the sliding glass door to the backyard. It wasn't a real backyard. It was a condo backyard, with just enough dirt and grass to give the impression of a backyard. Parallel brick fences ran from the sides of the condo to an attached building. I crossed the yard in three strides and stepped into the semi-attached garage.

I flipped a light switch, and a dusty bulb over the doorway sputtered to life.

The garage was mostly empty, apparently primarily used to house Jarred's truck. There was a washer and a dryer and a folded up ping-pong table. The table was covered with cobwebs. Damn waste. Next to the ping-pong table was a dartboard bristling with plastic red and yellow fletches. Boxes were stacked here and there.

I decided to check the boxes stacked here, rather than there, and within minutes sweat was dripping steadily from my brow and I felt as if I were being slowly cooked to death in this sweat box of a garage. I imagined my corpse being found hours from now, baked to perfection.

Most of the boxes were filled with books. Others were home to black widow spiders. I shuddered. Enough with the spiders, already. I stood there in the garage, hands on hips, wondering if I was barking up the wrong Joshua tree.

Maybe Willie Clarke really did run out of gas. And maybe Jarred had nothing to do with it.

Maybe.

I needed a better plan. There were too many boxes. And certainly too many spiders. If Jarred had indeed sabotaged Willie's truck, how would he have done it?

Standing in the middle of the garage, I closed my eyes. Sweat trickled down my spine. Hell, sweat trickled down *everywhere*.

I pictured Jarred heading back up to Willie's truck. Pictured Jarred using the keys to unlock Willie's truck door. Pictured Jarred stealing the bottles of water and cell phone. Pictured Jarred using a siphon hose, sucking on one end, getting the gas flowing, and nervously standing there in the desert while the precious fuel pumped out. Pictured Jarred using some of the water from the bottles to clean out the siphon hose. Pictured Jarred putting the empty bottles and the hose and a cell phone into a...what?

I opened my eyes.

A gym bag. At least, that's what I would have used.

I would have ditched the gym bag in the desert, but Jarred had Patricia with him. So the gym bag probably went home with him. Where it has stayed because the last thing Jarred expected was a search of his home.

I scanned the garage again. There, on some plastic storage shelves in the far corner, was a red gym bag.

I sucked in some air and, mentally preparing myself for the possibility of more black widows, crossed the length of the garage, pulled down the gym bag. I set it on some boxes and opened it.

Inside were two empty one-gallon bottles of Arrowhead water, a five-foot length of garden hose cut on both ends, and a cell phone. I flipped open the cell phone, turned it on, waited. Music chimed. It still had one bar of battery power left.

Using my own phone, I dialed Willie Clark's number. My finger shook while I dialed. When finished, I pressed send. More shaking. I sucked in some hot air, waited.

Waited.

The phone in my hand came to life, vibrating and ringing.

42.

I met Detective Sherbet at a McDonald's in downtown Fullerton across the street from the local junior college. The Fighting Hornets, or something. Half the customers who weren't Fighting Hornets were fighting mothers with kids. I came back carrying a tray filled with burgers and fries and sugar cookies to the table we had staked out in the corner of the dining area.

"Sugar cookies?" said Sherbet.

"With sprinkles," I said. "The sprinkles, of

course, do not imply I am a homosexual."

Sherbet started on the fries. He ate three at a time, mashing them together to form one huge super fry. Grease glistened between his thumb and forefingers.

"Why would you say something like that?" he asked.

I shrugged. "Seems to be a concern of yours."

He shook his head. "Now don't go bringing up my kid again."

"How's the kid?"

"Asshole," he said. "The kid's just fine. In fact, I gave up his neighborhood singing and dancing recital this evening to meet you, so this better be good."

"Singing recital?"

Sherbet shrugged, looked a little embarrassed. "It's a sort of one-man show. Or a one-kid show. And the kid's pretty good. Draws a fairly large neighborhood crowd. Stages it in our garage. He bakes cookies with his mother all afternoon, and serves them to anyone who shows up. It's quite a production."

"He'll be disappointed you're not there."

Sherbet stopped eating. "Yeah, he will be."

"Maybe I should make this quick," I said.

He sighed. "Yeah," he said. "Maybe you should."

"You love that kid."

"Yup."

"Even though he's not like you."

"I do. Would be easier if he were more like me."

"It's okay that he's not. Still your boy."

Sherbet was about to speak when I jumped in. "Let me guess: you want to change the subject."

"Lord, yes." His fries were gone, and he started in on the Big Mac. "So what do you have for me?"

"I might just have a killer for you," I said. In fact, I *knew* I had a killer for him, but I couldn't let on to Sherbet that I had broken into Jarred's condo. My search was illegal and would raise questions about evidence tampering. Jarred could walk. And I could lose my P.I. license.

"Okay, I'm interested," he said. "Tell me about it."

So I did.

Sherbet listened silently, working on his Big Mac, taking surprisingly delicate bites for someone who ate his fries three at a time. When I was done, he snorted. "Even though this Jarred went back for some water, doesn't mean he sabotaged the vehicle."

"Sure," I said. "But it gives Jarred opportunity. And since Willie Clarke was later found without his water, or his cell phone for that matter, there is some room for doubt."

Sherbet mulled this over, staring at me, chewing. The detective had me by about twenty years, but his face was smooth, nearly wrinkle free. His eyes never stopped working, as if he were continually sizing me up. There was grease on his chin, which caught some of the light and gleamed brilliantly.

"Sure, I'll give you that. If this kid, Willie, brings some water out, there should be some evidence of the bottles. I can tell you there was none. Kid brings his cell phone, he should have it; he didn't. Kid buys gas, he should have some; he didn't." Sherbet paused. "Don't forget he was also found nearly ten miles from his truck. Could have tossed both the empty water bottles and the dead cell phone, and ten miles of desert is a lot of heat and sand to search for a fucking cell phone and some plastic water containers."

"Two gallons of water should have gotten him to the main road," I said. "Or at least kept him alive long enough for a passing vehicle to spot him."

"Sure, if he didn't get lost first and waste the water."

"We are going in circles," I said. "Dancing."

"We are not dancing," he said defensively.

"What else do you have?"

"The way Jarred appeared that Saturday morning unannounced. The way he changed his tune once he returned from Willie's truck. The way he refused to go back to see if Willie was okay." I was leaning forward, my food completely forgotten. A few tables down a student was doing homework with some headphones on, a white cord attached to an iPod sitting on his table. "Taken individually, yes, sounds like I'm reaching for straws. Taken as a whole, we might have something here."

"Okay, so we might have something here. What's Jarred's motive for sabotage and murder?"

I shrugged. "Notoriety and prestige."

"Notoriety and prestige?" he said dubiously. A crumb had fallen from his mouth and disappeared into his thick arm hair. I wondered how many other crumbs had been lost in there. "That doesn't make sense."

"Not to you or me, but to Jarred it makes perfect sense. He is a young historian with something to prove. He staked out Rawhide as his very own. He was going to make a name for himself there, even if that name was only known in very limited circles."

"Have you been to Rawhide?"

"Yes."

"It ain't much."

"No. But it's untapped history."

Sherbet was done eating. He wadded up the Big Mac wrapper, sat back and folded his arms over his rotund belly. The plastic bench creaked under his weight. "So he offs his competitor."

"Yes."

"So what do you want from me?"

"I want you to dust Willie Clarke's truck for prints."

He shook his great head. "Of course there will be prints, Knighthorse. Jarred admitted to going back for water. They're probably all over the doors."

"Sure," I said.

Sherbet thought about it some more, and then the light went on. "The gas cap."

"Bingo," I said.

43.

I was on my back doing crunches behind my desk when the cell rang. Not missing a beat, I reached inside my pocket, removed the phone and flipped it open.

"Knighthorse."

"What the hell's wrong with you?" said Sherbet.

"I'm doing crunches."

"Crunches?"

"It's not easy being beautiful."

He ignored me. "We got the search warrant."

I stopped crunching, lay flat on the floor. "Go on."

"Jarred's prints were all over that goddamn gas cap, not to mention along the center console."

"Where the cell phone might have been located."

"Exactly."

"So when are you going in?" I asked.

"Tonight, when he gets home. He needs to be there for the search to be valid."

"Of course."

"But you knew that," he said.

"Yes."

"Sorry. I forget some private dicks know their shit."

"This one does."

He was quiet. I waited. I could hear him breathing.

"And Knighthorse?"

"Yes."

"Please tell me we won't find your prints at the condo."

"You won't find my prints at the condo."

"Good. Have you been there?"

"In passing."

Sherbet paused. If I listened closely enough I could hear his mustache lifting and falling with each breath. "In your expert opinion,

Knighthorse, is there anywhere in particular we should look once we get there?"

"If I were conducting the search, I would focus on the garage. Of course, that's just my expert opinion."

"Of course," he said. "Anything else?"

"I figure if he siphoned the gas, he would need a hose, and if he stole the water jugs, he would need somewhere to stash them."

"Like a bag?"

"Would be my guess."

J.R. RAIN

44.

Sanchez, Jesus and I were at a Baskin Robbins near Anaheim Stadium, or whatever the stadium is called these days. I had printed out three free child scoop coupons from the internet, courtesy of a major web page celebrating its fifth anniversary. We waited twenty minutes in line along with dozens of other customers, each holding similarly printed coupons. Sanchez folded his up and put it in his pocket. I think he was embarrassed. I didn't care. Free ice cream!

Afterward, sitting at a heavily dented metallic table, Sanchez examined his child scoop of rocky road, holding the cone daintily between his thumb and forefinger. "We spent twenty minutes in line for this?"

"Yeah," I said, "Isn't it great?"

Sanchez snorted.

Jesus said, "I think it's cool."

"Good kid," I said. "Besides, beggars can't be choosers."

"I'm not a beggar," said Sanchez. "I happen to have a real job with a steady income."

"Steady income is overrated. Where's the adventure?"

Sanchez shook his head. "The kid moved."

"Which kid?"

"The last kid on the list."

"But we saw him just last week at church."

"Yeah, well, now he lives in Florida with his grandparents."

I looked at Jesus, who was just finishing off his single mint and chip child scoop. "So you ran him out of town," I said to him.

Jesus shrugged. He was concentrating on the last of his ice cream. "I still owe him. He can run but he can't hide."

I said to Sanchez, "Are we buying plane tickets to Florida?"

"No. We're going to let this one slide."

"Big of you," I said.

"I still owe him," said Jesus.

"Not so big of him," I said.

"Hey, I'm only twelve."

"And what have you learned from all of this?" I asked.

Jesus shrugged, and started crunching on the waffle cone. I had finished mine in precisely three bites, as had Sanchez, who dropped his big hand on his kid's shoulders. "Answer him."

"One girlfriend at a time," said Jesus. He sounded as if this were a terrible punishment.

I said, "You do realize there are some guys who go their entire junior high and high school years without having a single girlfriend?"

"I know. I feel sorry for them." Jesus looked at me, grinning. "I mean, I feel sorry for you."

I looked at Sanchez. "You told him?"

"Hey, I was trying to make the same point. You just happened to come up."

"Thanks."

"Hey, I used you because the kid happens to look up to you," said Sanchez. "Why, I'll never know."

Jesus said, "You really never had a single girlfriend?"

"Girls are trouble," I said. "Besides, I had plenty in college."

"But I think girls are fun—"

"Not too much fun," said Sanchez, looking at his kid.

"No, dad."

"I was busy in high school," I said.

"What could be more important than girls?"

"Football."

"I played football in high school, too," said Sanchez, shrugging. "And I had girlfriends. No big deal."

"I took football seriously."

"So did I."

"I wanted to play in the pros," I said. "I had a plan. Girls would just get in the way."

"But that's the idea," said Sanchez. "Girls are made to get in the way. Sometimes it's nice when they get in the way."

"Right on, dad," said Jesus. He raised his hand. "High five."

Sanchez left him hanging. "But you made an exception for Cindy."

I said, "Cindy just happened to be the most special girl in the world."

"I think Cindy's hot," said Jesus, and Sanchez elbowed his kid hard enough to nearly knock him out of his seat.

"So do I," I said. "So do I."

45.

I was in my office with my feet up on my antique mahogany desk, careful of the gold-tooled leather top, re-reading Nietzsche's *Thus Spake Zarathustra*, when two things happened simultaneously: Jarred appeared in my office doorway pointing a rifle at my forehead, and my desk phone started ringing.

I did what any rational human being would in the presence of a ringing phone. I answered it.

Sherbet was on the other line. "We're

outside Jarred's condo. He never showed."

"No shit," I said.

Jarred kicked the door shut behind him and stepped deeper into my office. He quickly scanned the office, keeping the rifle on me. It was an old fashioned Colt .22. The kind one would find in a place like Rawhide, which is probably where Jarred got it.

Sherbet asked, "Any idea where he might be?"

"A fairly good one," I said.

"Then where is he?"

"Take a guess."

Jarred was walking around the desk, keeping the rifle on my face.

"He's with you," Sherbet said.

"Good guess."

"You need help?"

"Probably not."

"But it wouldn't be a bad idea."

"If you insist," I said.

"I'll send a car around."

At that moment, Jarred yanked the phone cord out of the wall. The line went dead. "Have a good day," I said, and hung up.

"Who the fuck was that?"

"Grandma," I said. "She tends to worry about me."

"She should worry about you, because you

are fucked, Knighthorse. Fucked. Do you understand me? Fucked!"

"If I'm hearing you correctly," I said, "I appear to be fucked."

"Put your hands flat on the desk where I can see them."

He caught me. I was inching toward my desk drawer, where I kept my Browning. I sighed, rested both hands on the tooled leather top of the desk.

"The oils from my palms might stain the tooled leather top of my desk."

"Fuck your desk."

Jarred had a sort of wild-eyed look about him. The sort of look my teammates had before big games, a look fueled by a lot of adrenaline and nerves and the certainty that you were going to hurt a lot of people in a few hours. Or be hurt. Jarred was still wearing his Rawhide-issued red cowboy shirt and jeans. He was sweating through his cowboy shirt. Must have gotten himself pretty worked up on the drive out here. His thinning hair was disheveled and his glasses had slid to the tip of his sweating nose. He didn't push them back up.

"They were waiting for me outside my condo," he said, spitting the words at me.

"They?"

He shoved the gun in my face, just inches

from my nose. I could smell the gun oil, could see faint scratches along the steel barrel. "Don't fuck with me, Knighthorse. The cops. The cops were waiting for me." He snapped the gun away and started pacing in front of my desk, keeping the gun loosely on me. Jarred looked insane. He was sweating profusely now. Swallowing repeatedly. "Patty told me you spoke to her the other day. She must have told you something."

"She told me you went back to the truck for water."

"Nothing wrong with that."

"Except we have your prints on the gas cap, Jarred."

"What do you mean?"

"We know you sabotaged the truck."

He looked at me from over his glasses. Sweat dripped from the tip of his nose, landed on my tooled leather. I would have to wipe that clean later. For now, I had bigger fish to fry.

"Give me the gun, Jarred."

"I can't."

"If you shoot me, you get the death penalty."

"Maybe that wouldn't be so bad."

I shrugged. "Where you stand now, a good lawyer talks the D.A. down to second degree murder."

Jarred was shaking. I could literally see the sweat spreading from under his armpits.

"I didn't kill anyone."

"Say that to Willie Clarke."

Jarred dropped into the client chair opposite me. The gun was pointed away from me. If I wanted to, I could lunge across the desk and wrestle it away from him. I wasn't in the lunging mood. Besides, I didn't think it would come to that.

"I didn't mean to kill him."

I said nothing.

"I just did it to scare him away, you know?" He paused, ran his hand through his hair. "I gambled on Rawhide. I visited there as a kid and fell in love with it. It stayed with me all these years."

"Maybe it's the cowboy in you."

He ignored me. I was used to being ignored. He continued. "So when I was casting around for a theme for my masters, Rawhide naturally came to mind. It was a good fit. I had a true love for American history, in particular Western history. I did some research and discovered nothing of any significance had been done on the town, and I knew I had found my purpose. I sold my condo in Boston, moved out west. I've poured my heart and soul into that little town."

"And then in waltzes Willie Clarke."

Jarred instinctively gripped the weapon in his lap. "He was fresh out of graduate school, but there was a sort of—"

"Cockiness?" I offered.

"Yes. A cockiness to him that I found infuriating. Which is probably why I don't like you."

"Sometimes I don't like me, either."

"Seriously?"

"No; I love me."

Jarred rolled his eyes. I think he might have thought about swinging his gun up to my face again, but decided against it. "Willie sounded so confident, so fucking sure of himself. As if he really thought he could unearth Sly's identity."

"Can't have that."

"Sly was mine," he hissed.

"If anyone was going to discover Sly's identity," I said, helping, "it would be you."

His eyes sparkled. "Yes! Exactly. Sly's one of the West's most intriguing mysteries."

"So you removed the threat. The threat being Willie."

"Hell, what the fuck was I supposed to do?"

"Not kill him. Work together. Share the glory."

Jarred was shaking his head. "I worked too hard and long to do that. Still, I didn't mean to kill him. I just wanted to scare him. I didn't want him to come back."

"Sure," I said. "You scared him to death."

A shadow crossed under my doorway. The

cavalry was here. Any minute now, they were going to barge in here, probably knock my door off its newly restored hinges. I couldn't let that happen.

"Give me the gun, Jarred."

He pushed his glasses up higher on his nose; they promptly slipped back down. He looked at me. His eyes were wide and reddish, perhaps irritated by his sweat. "I can't go to jail. Father would be very disappointed in me."

More shadows. It was going to get ugly in here. And I was still scrubbing the last of the bloodstains out of my carpet.

"He's very renowned, you know. Teaches at Princeton. He didn't approve of me coming out to Rawhide. Thought it was beneath us. Thought it was a mistake."

"Boy was he wrong," I said.

Jarred gave me a half smile and pushed his glasses up. "They're coming for me, aren't they?"

I kept my eyes on him and nodded my head slowly. I didn't like the tone his voice had suddenly taken on. Somber and distant, a voice empty of hope.

"You were talking to the police earlier, weren't you?" he asked.

"Just give me the gun, Jarred."

"I think...not."

"They'll shoot you."

"Now there's a thought," he said. "Would make things a lot easier, wouldn't it? My parents would be disgraced, sure. But at least the matter will be done with short and quick."

"Don't do this, Jarred. It's not worth it."

"Not worth it? Oh, I think it is." He looked at me, smiled. Pushed his glasses up. His eyes weren't right. His lower lip trembled. "Tell my dad to fuck off for me."

"Tell him yourself."

"Later, Knighthorse."

He swung the rifle around and, in a practiced motion, stuck the muzzle in his mouth and pulled the trigger.

46.

It was a week later.

Cindy and I were in bed together, where we belonged, watching the local nightly news. Ginger the dog was burrowed under the covers between my ankles. Now, after twenty-five minutes of grisly murders, missing kids and reports of unsafe foods and medicines, came the feel-good story of the day—wrapped around, of course, another murder.

There, on Cindy's 19" TV screen in her cozy bedroom was Jones T. Jones's hawkish face and gold hoop earrings.

Jones was standing in front of Ye Olde Curiosity Shoppe, before a crowd of reporters. For the cameras, Jones ditched the cheesy used car salesman facade and adopted a more somber expression and tone. Peppering his speech liberally with references to his store, Jones announced that with the help of private investigator Jim Knighthorse—yes that Jim Knighthorse of football fame—they had not only uncovered the name of the mummy, but his original murderer.

The camera cut to a young male Asian field reporter, who then went on to explain, in a butchered and confusing summary, the role that Tafford Barron's ancestor, yes that Tafford Barron who is currently running for a House seat, had had in the murder of Boonie Adams.

"You were mentioned on the news!" Cindy squealed, turning off the TV. "And in a non-football capacity. I'm so impressed."

"Impressed enough to sleep with me?"

"What the hell do you call what we just did thirty minutes ago?"

"Not sleeping."

Ginger shifted positions and pressed her cold nose into my anklebones. I shivered involuntarily.

"I don't like this Jones T. Jones chap," said Cindy. "He reminds me of a used car salesman."

"He's worse than that," I said. "He's selling dead men. So to speak."

"Oh, yuck."

Ginger raised her head. I knew this because a section of the comforter between my feet rose up. It dropped back down a moment later.

"Business is already picking up," I said. "And I just received my final check from Jones. Want to go to Sir Winston's?"

She shook her head. "Too snooty."

I hugged her tightly. "My kind of gal."

"So what are you going to do with the bonus?"

"Take you to dinner. Buy you pearls and diamonds."

"Or get caught up on your bills."

"Or that," I said. "Or I could always use it to start a new life in the Bahamas. Maybe run a juice bar on the beach."

"Can I come?"

"Only if I can refer to you as my bikini babe."

"Deal," she said, then frowned.

"Something I said?"

"No. It's this Jones T. Jones character. Just doesn't seem right that he's still profiting from Boonie's murder."

"I agree," I said. "Which is why I took the liberty to research Boonie's kin."

"You didn't."

"I did."

"Judging by that smug grin on your face, I would say that you found them."

"I did. Or some of them who still happen to live in Barstow. I suggested to them that Boonie should receive a decent burial with his family present. And they agreed. One old lady, a great great granddaughter, actually cried."

"And what does Jones T. Jones think of this?"

"Oh, he won't like it at first, but he'll cave in, and work the funeral into a huge propaganda stunt. Believe me, in the end, Jones will have profited very well from Boonie's murder."

"Speaking of which, explain to me again what happened to Boonie's killer. The news sort of jumbled it."

"A hundred and twenty years ago, young Johanson Barron gets in a barroom fight with Boonie Adams, stabbing Boonie in the shoulder. A week later Johanson somehow lures Boonie out into the desert, shoots him and leaves him to die. A month later, the Barron family, perhaps aware of this killing, quietly ships Johanson out of Rawhide, where he eventually winds up in Dodge City. Where, I might add, he eventually hangs for a different murder two years later. So justice was served, so to speak."

"How do you know all this?"

"I happen to be an ace detective," I said. "That, and I had the help of Rawhide's newest curator, one Patricia McGovern."

"Will this somewhat scandalous news hurt Tafford Barron's chances of running for Congress?"

"One can only hope," I said. "A good spin doctor can probably get him out of this scrap, but we'll see."

"Did you eventually find Jarred's father?"

"I did."

"Did you relay the message?"

"It was a dying man's last request," I said. "What else could I do?"

"Was it hard for his father to hear?"

"He broke down crying, so I think so."

"Like pouring salt in the wound," said Cindy.

"Yes," I said.

"But you had to do it," she said.

"Yes."

Street sounds came from below, especially the sound of a loud muffler. In fact, I heard it pass on several occasions. As it was coming again, I got up out of bed, padded across her hardwood floor, and glanced out her third story window in time to see an older model white BMW chug slowly down the street. Black exhaust spewed from the muffler. I frowned.

"You okay?" Cindy asked.

"Yes."

"What is it?"

"Nothing," I said, and came back to bed.

"So tell me," said Cindy, snuggling against me, her breath hot on my neck. "Was it Jarred who shot at you in the desert?"

"We'll never know for sure, but I think it's a safe bet. A Rawhide maintenance truck was getting serviced not too far from where we had met for lunch. He could have easily swapped vehicles."

"Why bother swapping vehicles if his intent was killing you?" Cindy asked. "With you dead, there would be no witnesses."

I shrugged. "In case he didn't kill me; in case there was a witness."

"I've never had anyone shoot at me," she said, shuddering under the covers. "I would be terrified."

"At first, but then survival supercedes fear."

We were silent some more. Ginger snored contentedly between my ankles. A helluva heating pad.

"Do you think you'll coach again next year?" Cindy asked.

Our team had played its final game tonight. We finished the season on a high note, winning by a huge margin, the biggest in quite some time. In fact, we had won four of the last five games, which, coincidentally, was when I was hired on as an assistant coach. Coach Swanson had asked me back next year.

"I told him I would think about it," I said.

"But I thought you really enjoyed it."

"Oh, I do. But a coach needs to give more of himself. Hell, most coaches commit their lives to their teams."

"You were busy with the mummy, and with my stalker."

"Of which, one is still on the loose," I said.

"What's his name?"

"Chad Schwendinger," I said. "No wonder he turned out bad."

"I'm not worried," she said. "I have my big strong man to protect me."

I was quiet, thinking about the stalker, about coaching, about the mummy, about my mommy. And through it all, I mostly thought about having a beer.

"Maybe next year I can take some time off from detecting to coach."

"You look like a coach. Did I ever tell you that? The kids look up to you. I was watching them tonight. They were hanging onto your every word down there on the sideline."

"I think everyone should hang onto my every word."

"I know you do," said Cindy. "Speaking of your word, are you ever going to ask me to marry you?"

"Yes."

"When?"

"When I'm out of debt."

She was silent, meditative. She stroked my bicep. "I would also want you to stop drinking before we're married."

I nodded, but said nothing. Damn, I wanted a drink. Now.

"Maybe you need help," she offered.

"Probably."

"But you don't want to get it."

"I like drinking," I said.

"So you would rather get drunk than marry me?"

"I want both."

"You can't have both, Jim. You need to make a decision."

I turned and faced her, our noses touching. I inhaled deeply. She was staring up at me, the whites of her eyes luminescent. "There is no decision to make. I won't lose you again. But can we give this a little time?"

She burrowed her face into the crook of my neck and kissed me softly.

"Yes," she said sleepily. "We can give it a

little time."

47.

Cindy spent the next few minutes flinching spasmodically into sleep. When she was snoring softly, I eased out of bed and padded quietly into the kitchen and opened the fridge door and removed a cold can of the thing that had been obsessively raging through my thoughts for the last hour. And it wasn't a Diet Coke.

Cindy allowed me to keep a case of beer at her house, as long as I didn't go through it too quickly.

That, of course, was the challenge.

So I was sitting in the darkness at the kitchen table working on my third Miller Light, contemplating a fourth, when I heard the familiar rumble of the muffler. I parted the curtains and looked down onto the street below as the same older model BMW pulled up along the curb, stopping in the shadows just outside a splash of lamplight.

I sipped from the can, stared down. I forgot about wanting a fourth beer.

The driver killed the engine and the lights. The tinted window rolled down and a man's pale face appeared. If I wasn't mistaken, as his jawline caught some of the diluted street light, he was looking up at Cindy's condo.

I finished the beer and spent the next ten minutes staring down into the small squarish window three floors below, staring so hard that sometimes the window blurred into a hazy black amorphous mass. Luckily, blinking remedied this problem.

I watched it some more, and decided it was time for a chat. I pulled on a light jacket, because even I get cold, and stepped out of the condo and into the cool night air. I worked my way between the rows of condos, through a security gate and out toward the street.

Once there, I saw that the driver had stepped out of the car and was now rummaging through the trunk. The trunk lid blocked his face. Below the corner of the rear fender, and glowing slightly in the diluted street light, I could see a pair of dirty sneakers. Whoever he was withdrew something from his trunk and set it by his feet.

Light reflecting dully off its plastic surface, it looked vaguely like a slightly deflated football, if footballs had handles and spouts.

Gas can.

Pale hands reached up for trunk lid. Shut it softly.

And I found myself looking into the face of a very shocked, very heavy-set middle-aged man with a thick head of receding hair. Sort of the Roger Staubach look. He was wearing a black Members Only jacket and black sweats, as any good stalker should. He couldn't have looked more startled, eyes bulging and mouth working.

"Run out of gas?" I asked.

The look of astonishment quickly turned into something ugly. He bared his teeth and reached inside his jacket, shouting: "Darwin is the devil."

But before he could remove his hand, I pushed off the fender and punched him full in the face. His arms windmilled, flinging what appeared to be a gun into the nearby bushes. He collapsed straight to the ground.

"Only in the bedroom," I said. "A devil only in the bedroom."

He held his face and moaned and bled. I rolled him over and removed his wallet from his back pocket, hoping against hope I had gotten the right man. And I had. Chad Schwendinger. Hell of a name.

No wonder he turned out bad.

48.

Yesterday, in a small desert town called Apple Valley, ol' Boonie was finally put to rest amid much fanfare. Jones T. Jones was there. He even shed a tear, which may or may not have been legit. Anyway, I thought he was going to miss his mummy. They had gotten along so well together.

I was still drinking too much, but that was not insurmountable. That was fixable, and someday when I had put my own mother's murder to rest, I would put my drinking to rest, too. And then I would ask a certain someone to marry me.

But first things first.

A door to my right opened and a bespectacled young man with no chin poked his head out. He was dressed in a white lab coat. "It's ready, Mr. Knighthorse."

"How did it turn out?"

"Great, I think. You can thank the marvels of modern technology."

So I followed him in. Took a seat next to a flat-screen computer monitor that was turned away from me.

"Here you go," he said. And turned the monitor toward me. "Twenty years, just like you asked."

On the screen before me was the headshot of a white Caucasian male of about forty. I leaned a little closer, aware that my beating heart had increased in tempo, thudding dully in my skull. The man on the screen had not aged well. His face was weathered from too many years in the sun and surf. His blond hair was turning a dirty blond, almost gray. Blue eyes and white teeth.

It's called age progression technology, and it's used to identify runaways and kidnap victims. The man on the screen before me was the eighteen-year-old kid from the pier, the kid who had taken an interest in my mother. Except in the age progression photograph, he wasn't a kid anymore. He was a man. An older man who clearly loved to surf and still lived in Huntington Beach. An older man with three adorable kids who loved their grandfather. An older man who was the son of the homicide detective who investigated my mother's murder.

"I hope this helps," said the technician.

I was finding breathing difficult.

"Are you okay?" asked the technician.

The room was turning slowly. From somewhere very far away, I heard the technician ask again if I was okay.

I felt sick and stumbled out of the small room and found the nearest bathroom and threw up my lunch and breakfast. I flushed the toilet and sat on the seat and wiped my mouth with the back of my hand and tried to control my breathing.

I sat like that for a very long time.

The End

Knighthorse returns in:
Hail Mary
by J.R. Rain
Available now!

About the Author:

J.R. Rain is an ex-private investigator who now writes full-time. He lives in a small house on a small island with his small dog, Sadie. Please visit him at www.jrrain.com.

Made in the USA
Middletown, DE
29 December 2022

20578931R00161